W9-BTC-743

SCAR VEGAS

and other stories

TOM PAINE

Harcourt, Inc.
New York   San Diego   London

MIDDLEBURY COLLEGE LIBRARY

Copyright © 2000 by TLP, Inc.

All rights reserved. No part of this publication may be
reproduced or transmitted in any form or by any means,
electronic or mechanical, including photocopy, recording,
or any information storage and retrieval system, without permission
in writing from the publisher.

Requests for permission to make copies of any part of the work
should be mailed to: Permissions Department, Harcourt, Inc.,
6277 Sea Harbor Drive, Orlando, Florida 32887-6777.

The author wishes to thank the Corporation of Yaddo.

Library of Congress Cataloging-in-Publication Data
Paine, Tom.
Scar Vegas:global stories/Tom Paine.
p.   cm.
Contents: Will you say something, Monsieur Eliot?—General
Markman's last stand—Scar Vegas—Unapproved minutes of the
Carthage, Vermont, Zoning Board of Adjustment—The spoon
children—The hotel on Monkey Forest Road—Ceauşescu's cat—
The mayor of St. John—A predictable nightmare on the eve of the
stock market breaking 6,000—The battle of Khafji.
ISBN 0-15-100489-7
I. Title.
PS3566.A342S33   2000
813'.54—dc21   99-16416

Text set in Fairfield Light
Designed by Lydia D'moch

Printed in the United States of America
A C E F D B

Publication acknowledgments appear on page vii,
which constitutes a continuation of the copyright page.

for
Ken Saro-Wiwa
Nigerian writer and activist
hanged for our insatiable oil gluttony
November 20, 1995

"If we can get the oppressors out of the way,
if we can get the pollution to stop,
I am sure Ogoni would be a happy land."

Contents

Will You Say Something, Monsieur Eliot?   1

General Markman's Last Stand   18

Scar Vegas   40

Unapproved Minutes of the Carthage, Vermont,
Zoning Board of Adjustment   59

The Spoon Children   76

The Hotel on Monkey Forest Road   96

Ceauşescu's Cat   124

The Mayor of St. John   146

A Predictable Nightmare
on the Eve of the Stock Market Breaking 6,000   171

The Battle of Khafji   192

Publication Acknowledgments

"Will You Say Something, Monsieur Eliot?" was originally published in *The New Yorker,* October 4, 1994, and *Prize Stories: The O. Henry Awards,* 1996.

"General Markman's Last Stand" originally appeared in *Story,* Summer 1995, and in *New Stories from the South,* 1996.

"Scar Vegas" originally appeared in *The Oxford American,* Summer 1996, and in *The 1998 Pushcart Prize XXII.*

"Unapproved Minutes of the Carthage, Vermont, Zoning Board of Adjustment" was first published by *Harper's,* April 1998.

"The Spoon Children" originally appeared in *Zoetrope,* Fall 1997.

"Ceauşescu's Cat" was first published by *The New England Review,* Summer 1999.

"The Mayor of St. John" was originally published in *American Fiction X: The Best Stories from Unpublished Writers,* March 1999.

"The Battle of Khafji" originally appeared in *Playboy* magazine, January 1998, and as "From Basra to Bethlehem" in *Seven Days,* 1996, and *The 1997 Pushcart Prize XXI.*

Will You Say Something, Monsieur Eliot?

AFTER THE EYE passed over, the shivering Concordia yawl *Bliss* was picked up and tossed sideways down into a trough. For a moment in the dark that had been a brilliant noon two hours earlier Eliot saw a light on the horizon and knew it was the light at the top of his own mast. The light flickered and went black, and there was nothing but the white noise of the storm. The wooden yawl shuddered deep in her timbers, and Eliot was catapulted from the cockpit and landed chin first on the deck and heard his molars shatter. Weightless for a moment as *Bliss* dropped, Eliot again cracked down against the deck like a fish. The bow rose up the face of a mountain of water and Eliot fell headfirst toward the wheel. His heavy arms locked in the spokes, and his Adam's apple crunched on mahogany, and he was upside down, bare feet to the sky. *Bliss* paused at the crest before her bow came down hard, hurtling Eliot backward through the companionway onto the teak floor below, where he rolled in a soup of seawater and motor oil and caulking.

The creaking of the hull planks rose to a moan and subsided and rose again. The garboard plank was wrenching away from the keel, and the sea overwhelming the pumps. Eliot caught his breath and lifted his head. The storm paused. In the pause Eliot heard a distant *plink*, the single sharp piano *plink* of the lower shroud snapping, and then the crack of the main mast as it folded at its midsection into the sea. *Bliss* rose and twisted against the storm. The seaborne mast buffeted, a battering ram still wired to the hull. Eliot was braced against the sink in the galley reaching for the bolt cutters when the mast rammed through the after hull. He crawled behind the companionway toward the hole with a red flotation cushion for a potential patch and a broken paddle for a wedge. The sea poured in against his knees. The mast broke through again, and Eliot was driven backward on a river into the cabin. He crawled to his feet and slid an orange life jacket over his head, and *Bliss* was thrown from the sea into the air and turned turtle and the sea rushed into the cabin and she righted again. Climbing up the companionway, Eliot saw in the west the vaporous glow of the end of the storm working toward him. He thrust his arms through the wheel and watched the light grow, and a rogue wave dropped from the heavens and drove *Bliss* down into the sea.

Eliot's shoulders and head bobbed in the sea like a red bottle. He was shirtless and stripped of his life jacket, and his face bloated from twenty-four hours of exposure and oozing from cuts and abrasions. His eyes were swollen half shut. The sharp nubs of his broken teeth lanced at his tongue and Eliot counted six—three to starboard and three to port. Once a dolphin flew out of the sea not far from Eliot, but it didn't come again, and the sea was mute. Eliot's lips fissured and the fissures spread red and raw. At night he watched the sky for a shooting star but never asked to be saved when he saw the first one, and there were dozens, as if every star in the sky were thrown down. He floated on his back all night and missed *Bliss* more than anyone because *Bliss* was perfection. Eliot exhaled and sank under, down to his blistered lips and nose, and when he filled his lungs the white island of his belly emerged, breaking the black surface, and he let the breath go in a gasp and sank down again and then pulled the night again into his lungs. It went on and on, this rising and falling. Morning pinched the stars from the sky one at a time, and Eliot watched them go, and slowly the gray turned to yellow and then gold, and the sun burned at the edge of the Atlantic Sea.

On the second day, Eliot saw something long and shiny in the sun, and he paddled to it. It was the boom of *Bliss*, yellow-varnished Sitka spruce rolling in the sea. Eliot removed his belt from the tight loops of his bunched shorts. He tied the belt around the boom and and looped his arm through the sling and fell back with a groan and hung in the water. He slid his burning face under the sea and looked up through its lens at a cloud quivering like mercury and blew silver bubbles to the surface. His face turned down toward the depths, and his puffy hand drifted before his face, and his Princeton ring sparkled gold in the airy blue. Eliot pointed downward and cried out with the last air in his lungs, and the cry warbled in the water, and his breath bubbled up his forehead. He broke the surface gasping and flopped up across the boom with his face in the sea. Eliot looked down into the water ten meters, where there was nothing, just liquid blue fading into black. He turned his head and sucked in a loud breath and searched the deserted sea. Skin shriveled off his shoulders and drifted down and away as Eliot held his breath and watched the sails of skin battered in the invisible eddies.

On the day before leaving for this single-handed sail—out of the Bahamas and bound for St. Barts—Eliot had stood over his secretary's desk with his bag over his shoulder and written a check for fifty thousand dollars. Eliot told her to send it to David Mercer at Fleet, with best regards. Eliot's tenth Princeton reunion was in June and he had been taunting David— threatening not to give any money this year—and one night was watching David squirm in his chair at the Princeton Club when David said out of the blue, What if something happened?

What if something happened when?

On your trip, David said. Your sailing trip.

Like what? Eliot said.

Like something could happen.

Like *what* could happen?

David raised his mineral water to his lips. Eliot, don't you see something could go wrong?

I've single-handed *Bliss* dozens of times.

So you're not afraid.

Not really.

You think it's impossible?

What?

You know.

I never think about that.

Never?

I think about dropping twenty pounds. Wasn't this dinner about money?

Eliot, do you mind my making a personal comment?

No more than usual.

That's kind of fucked.

Yes? You think so?

Yes. I do.

Let me tell you something, David.

I'm listening.

You won't understand this at all.

Say it, Eliot.

I don't really understand it myself.

Understand what?

The world loves me.

David stared at Eliot, and the waiter arrived and stood over their table, looking from one man to the other.

Ready to order, sirs?

David shook his head and rubbed at the creases in his brow. He looked at Eliot, who hadn't aged since Princeton.

Eliot finished his drink and looked up at the waiter and ordered another. The waiter nodded and turned to David, who looked at Eliot and repeated, *The world loves you?*

The waiter's gaze swiveled back to Eliot. Eliot laughed and shook his beautiful strawberry head. The laughter rolled up out of him as if he were a child being tickled.

What, said David. What's so funny?

The third day the sea was glass, and then the wind whispered at noon and feathered the glass in running swaths. For hours, Eliot watched the swaths dapple in the sun, and once a dolphin rose against the horizon. Eliot hooked the belt around his head, using it as a sling under his chin, and slept lightly for a few hours with his head against the boom. When he awoke, his throat was on fire, and he wanted to drink from the sea and he swallowed, and the salt burned like acid down his throat. Soon the sun was slipping away and the breeze blew cool on the burned skin of his face and shoulders. The sun dropped out of sight, and Eliot saw the green flash, and the green flash was a sure sign to him. When he closed his eyes he saw the solar phenomenon lingering like green lightning on the glowing red interior of his swollen eyelids.

Tomorrow, said Eliot, nodding to the universe with closed eyes.

At dawn, Eliot took the metal edge at the end of the belt and carved a line next to the other three scratches. He tried to think of something dramatic to scratch in the boom for posterity and could only think of adding his name, Eliot Swan. He closed his eyes and saw the boom over the fieldstone fireplace in the pastel living room of his house in Locust Valley and saw himself standing under it telling the story of his shipwreck. There were many people in the room listening, but they were all strangers. Eliot tried to picture the face of his former wife, Claudia, or his former partner, Clive, or one of his former mistresses, Ilena or Mandy, or his doubles partner, Henry, or his broker, Dutch, but Eliot could not recall a single face. For a moment Eliot thought he saw the face of the green-eyed Florentine waitress he was screwing when the sink broke and Claudia came in screaming and he went on pumping and laughing on the floor of the *gabinetto,* tossing Claudia all the lire in his pocket—but it wasn't the waitress, and Eliot gave up and opened his eyes.

———

The wind started after sunrise and whipped a spray off the tops of the waves. Eliot's boom bobbled against his bruised ribs, and he looked up at the clouds filling the sky. He cinched his belt tighter against the boom so there was no gap, and rode the slap and bounce of the agitated sea. The clouds darkened during the day and soon a low front appeared and sheeted across under the cumulus in long raked strips of black. A drizzle fell, and Eliot opened his mouth and drank as the drizzle became a downpour and then a wooden pounding of raindrops, filling his mouth as fast as he could swallow. Then the rain stopped as if a conductor had sliced his baton through the air and with his white-gloved hand swept away the clouds and calmed the sea.

Eliot felt the life from the rain pass into his wilting body, down his arms to his hands, and he ran his fingers through his hair. The strawberry hair came off in clumps and spread on the water. It floated with him and clung to his chest when he rose from the sea. Eliot loosened a canine tooth for hours with his tongue, and it fell out when he was face down in the water. It waggled through the chalky blue, sparkling in the shafts of underwater light until it winked and was swallowed by the dark below. Eliot ran his tongue over the bloody, wet crater until the taste of blood was gone and his mouth was dry and he smelled bile in his throat.

Eliot raised his chin to the setting sun.

Tomorrow then, he said.

Eliot heard voices—not the voices in the wind, but voices from a radio far away that faded and then crackled again. He heard a splashing sound and the creaking of timber and was sure it was a boat. He cried out, but there was nothing, not even the sound of the waves slapping against his boom. Eliot pulled on the boom and twisted his head slowly like a radar receiver. It was morning. He lowered his head and shielded his eyes with his forearm.

Eliot heard muffled foreign voices, and wood splashing in the water. He tried to call out, but his voice snapped and there was only a croaking. The boat's waves splashed toward him, and Eliot heard a jumble of voices overhead. The shadow of the bow fell over him, and his boom was banging against the boat.

Eliot felt feet on his shoulders and toes searching under his armpits. He reached upward slowly. His hands touched thin ankles but slid down and fell back into the water. The voices were loud now. Eliot clung to the boom. A rope fell on his head. Eliot raised his arms and understood and pulled the rough rope over his burned shoulders. He was dragged up the side of the boat, wood against his belly. A woman yelled and Eliot felt something sharp on the side of the boat catching his foot. The sharpness pulled deeply in the skin of his instep as he was yanked upward and Eliot scraped over the gunwale and flopped like a large dead fish onto the deck.

The sun burned through his blind eyes. There were yellow spots on the backs of his eyelids. The yellow broke up and scattered into a thousand small suns, and Eliot saw ideas whipping around his head as if in a hurricane, taunting him and then fading. A woman's voice was in his ear. There was a cloth and warm water, and she was wiping his eyes tenderly. The woman was singing a lullaby. The others were quiet while she sang in his ear and wiped his eyes. Her breath steamed on his ear. The boat creaked, but there was no motion on the deck.

Eliot tried to get up on his elbows. There was a clamor of voices, and he lay down again. Water was poured into his mouth and it curled warm down within him. Eliot felt a thumb

on his eyelid, pushing upward. His eyelid opened and Eliot saw
a yellow eye.

Monsieur, parlez-vous français?

The thumb held his eye open, and Eliot saw a black face
with cracked red lips and broken teeth. Eliot moved his head
to the side, releasing the thumb, and blinked. He rubbed his
eyes with his aching hands and he could see dozens of black
faces crowded over him, waiting silently. A man in a torn light-
blue shirt dress shirt with dirty white ruffles said, *Parlez-vous
français?*

Eliot opened his lips and said, I am American.

The faces turned to the short man with the ruffles and he
waved his hand like an impresario and pointed at Eliot and said
triumphantly, U.S.A.!

The faces, open-mouthed, looked down at Eliot, and the
man in the ruffles nodded like a king and pointed at him and
repeated, U.S.A.!

Their faces floated down to him and bobbed in the air, and
Eliot felt dozens of dry hot hands patting his belly. The old
woman who had sung the lullaby to him cried, her hands over
her face, and ran her wet palms lightly over his forehead. Eliot
saw many in the crowd make the sign of the cross and raise
their eyes to the heavens, and the man in the ruffled shirt cut
through the crowd and his face drifted down. He took Eliot's
hand and said, I am Alphonse.

Eliot.

Monsieur Eliot, said Alphonse. We are happy to see you
now.

Where are you from?

We are left from Haiti.

How long at sea?

We are at sea twenty days.

9

Does this boat sail?

There is a storm, Monsieur Eliot. We have no good sails. Shit.

We are very happy to see you now.

Eliot looked up at the mast and saw it was a telephone pole and the boom was a series of boards lashed together with black rope. A patchwork sail hung limp against the mast, and broken ropes hung loose like vines. The rough wood on the side of the boat was covered with the cryptic destinations of old shipping crates. Eliot could see the sea, flat and silent, through the cracks. A small boy with a large head pushed through the crowd and looked at Eliot and poured a bucket of dirty seawater over the side of the boat.

Alphonse looked down at Eliot and smiled.

Now we are saved, said Alphonse.

Eliot looked up at the empty blue sky, and for the first time it seemed foreign and unknown to him. He looked at it and closed his eyes and retreated into the shell of his body.

Because you are American, we are saved.

Alphonse took Eliot's hand in his own and pressed it to his heart. You have a big boat? said Alphonse.

She sank.

You are very rich?

Eliot said nothing, but his throat burned.

Alphonse spread his hands wide and his face snapped into a fiery grin. He turned and spoke rapidly in Creole to the other faces. All the Haitians spoke at once, and some of the old women raised their hands to the sky, and a few of the men cried.

Alphonse raised Eliot's hand and kissed his Princeton ring.

What did you tell them?

I tell them you are a rich American and very big in America and now the president of the United States will make them look for you and we are saved. They are very happy to hear this good news.

The Haitians hugged one another and scanned the horizon and beamed at Alphonse. Eliot looked up at the sky and closed his eyes.

The sea was light-blue ice. The sun was insolent and bitter. The Haitians were silent, sprawled on the burning wood of the deck as if struck down. They had placed Eliot on a platform in the center of the boat, and Alphonse had used his pale-blue shirt to rig an awning over Eliot's head. An old man grunted from the front of the boat, and other voices were praying with a sound like cicadas. A woman stood in the bow, fishing with a string. When Eliot moved his head he saw faces twitch and look up at him from the deck with expectation. The sail quivered occasionally as if possessed.

Eliot's right foot throbbed for the first two days. A nail sticking out of the planks on the side of the boat had gashed jagged and deep. A faded little girl came to look at Eliot and ran her soft fingers down the length of his body until she came to his foot, where she stopped and lowered her face and sniffed. She went back to Eliot's head and knocked on his skull lightly with her hand balled into a fist. Then she pointed to his toe and pinched her nose. The girl looked at Eliot and Eliot looked at the girl. Eliot turned his head, and Alphonse, who was always watching from nearby, where he squatted inside a cardboard box, stood slowly and hobbled over. Alphonse took Eliot's hand and pressed it to his chest and squinted at the horizon with his yellow eyes.

Alphonse, said Eliot.

Oui, Monsieur Eliot?

My foot is infected.

Alphonse looked at Eliot's foot and held it between his fingers and twisted it from side to side.

Monsieur Eliot, said Alphonse. It is not bad.

It *is* bad, said Eliot. It is infected.

Alphonse looked out across the sea, still holding Eliot's toe. You are big man in America, said Alphonse. They will come for you.

Alphonse let go of Eliot's foot and returned to his box. A wrinkled woman shuffled over and poured a few drops of water into Eliot's mouth from the good edge of a broken glass. A few minutes later a young girl carefully poured a few drops into his mouth from a rusty can. Alphonse watched them and nodded from his box. Eliot kept his mouth open, and one by one Haitians came to him and offered a few drops of their supply.

In the evening, the woman who had sung the lullaby in his ear hummed a song and laid her cool hand on Eliot's hot forehead and Eliot closed his eyes and nodded. She stopped and pulled back her hand and looked down at him and her hand in surprise. In the melody or the touch Eliot had remembered something, something as rare in his life as the green flash at sunset. Others came during the evening and spoke in Creole and touched his body, and sometimes they cried and wiped their tears on his chest. Alphonse came and took down the awning when it was dark and gave Eliot a few gulps of water. Then he went back to his box and watched Eliot look up at the stars.

On the fifth day no one brought him water, and he knew there was no water, and on the sixth day he heard the Haitians lying near him scuttle away. He knew it was the smell of his rotting foot. Alphonse stood over his foot and with his thumb traced the blue lines of poison up Eliot's calf to his knee. Eliot saw only a shimmering black form moving like liquid in the glare, but Eliot smelled the rot from his toe and had seen the blue lines of the poison creeping along his veins toward his heart.

Monsieur? said Alphonse.

Cut it off.

Monsieur, you know the Americans will come. He pointed out to sea.

Cut it off, said Eliot. Above the knee.

Non, non, Monsieur Eliot. We wait for tomorrow.

Do it today. You have a machete?

No, Monsieur, not today.

Alphonse.

Monsieur Eliot?

Take my ring.

Alphonse shook his head sharply and hobbled back to his box. The sun was eggshell blue through the shirt-awning above Eliot's head. The boat whispered with the sound of scorched lungs, and Eliot wanted to say he was a skeleton bleaching in the sun. Eliot did not understand. With his eyes closed, he saw the skeleton lying on the deck, bleached and white. He tried to open his eyes and hold them open, staring at the strange sky; he tried to count to a hundred, but when his eyes fell closed he saw the skeleton. At dusk Eliot turned his head to the side in time to see a dolphin leap and the sea flat again.

The first Haitian died on the night of the sixth day. Eliot heard grunting and a splash and turned his head to see Alphonse and another man leaning over the side of the boat. In the morning when the sky was still pink Eliot heard another splash, but before this splash there was a sharp shout and another shout from Alphonse in the box. Alphonse hobbled to his side and said, It is the husband of the woman from the night.

Alphonse took Eliot's hand, and Alphonse's head and face were red and on fire.

I love America, he said. I teach myself to speak English. I listen to English on the radio for many years. We make this boat. We go to America. My daughter with me. You will see, Monsieur Eliot.

Take off the leg, said Eliot.

Tomorrow, said Alphonse.

Alphonse, said Eliot. Take off the leg or I'll die.

If you die, Monsieur Eliot, many will die.

Alphonse.

They see you, Monsieur Eliot. You are here. *C'est un miracle.* The sea is big and you are here from America. *Un miracle.* You see?

I'm going to die.

You will not die, Monsieur Eliot. Many pray for you. Do you pray, Monsieur?

Shit.

Alphonse stayed with Eliot and held his hand through the day. The sun hammered, and there was no air. The smell of his foot was strong and the two of them wheezed through their mouths. Alphonse held Eliot's hand and sat exposed to the sun on the edge of the platform. In the afternoon Alphonse wet a rag on a string over the side of the boat and wiped Eliot's forehead. Alphonse emptied water from below over the side of the boat and hobbled around the boat every hour and whispered to the Haitians the word "America" and pointed at Eliot. At dusk, Alphonse brought a little girl no more than five to his side, holding her up from behind as if teaching her to walk, and she watched Eliot. Her ribs showed through her torn shirt. She looked up at Alphonse, who smiled, and the girl smiled, and Alphonse walked her away.

———

On the night of the seventh day, Eliot heard more bodies going over the side. Those that went with a splash and grunts Eliot knew were already dead, but many more went with a sucking sound and Eliot knew those had jumped, and some cried out and there was no question. Alphonse sat with Eliot all day on the eighth day and even found a few drops of water for his lips. On that night the bodies again jumped or were dropped over the side, and Alphonse came to him at dawn and held Eliot's foot gently in his hands.

How many on the boat? said Eliot.

I do not know. We are many.

How many? A hundred?

We are many. I know everyone. We are many, and many are family.

How many are gone?

They are gone, Monsieur. The others are alive.

How many?

Alphonse shrugged. It is too late for them. I pray for those who live.

The woman who had sung the lullaby to Eliot died at noon and was carried by three men to the side of the boat. Her body was rested on the railing and rolled slowly over the side, and her splash cut through the heat. The splash echoed in Eliot's skull and he closed his eyes and a green flash turned to black. Alphonse went to the railing and looked down at the sea and made the sign of the cross. A young woman with a scar on her nose stood on shaking legs in the center of the boat and sang in slow Creole. She swayed and sang with eyes closed, and other voices from the floor of the boat rose up in the sun. The woman collapsed after hanging like a puppet with a look of surprise.

Alphonse hobbled to her and he carried her in his arms and dropped her over the side of the boat. On the way back to his box he stopped and looked at his feet and said, My daughter.

Eliot closed his eyes.

Monsieur Eliot, my daughter.

Eliot turned his head away.

Alphonse sat with Eliot and cried with no tears and asked him to say something please about the President of the United States and how the boats would come to take them all to America.

Tell them, Monsieur Eliot. They believe you.

At night the Haitians flew over the side like black ghosts and Eliot heard their footsteps as they passed his platform and heard them go into the sea. Eliot heard the feet pass him and then the hands on the edge of the boat and only once a shout and a loud splash, and in the morning watched a body floating near the boat. A foot stuck up stiff in the air. Alphonse was sitting in his box with his face in his hands, and Eliot thought Alphonse was dead.

Eliot heard a fly. He tried to see the fly but he could not turn his head, and the sound of the fly grew louder. Eliot looked up, and the sound of the fly became the sound of an engine, and he heard the helicopter coming and the helicopter was right over his head, whooshing over the boat. The helicopter swung around again and blocked the sun. Eliot saw the American flag on the side. Two seamen in white helmets looked down from the wide door, and one waved. The men swung a net down to the boat with dozens of plastic jugs, and Eliot could feel feet moving on the boat toward the supplies. Eliot felt the cool wash from the blades. An aluminum gurney rocked down from the helicopter. Hands slipped him into the gurney, and it rose swinging in the air.

Eliot was pulled into the empty cave of the helicopter. The pilot turned his blue eyes to Eliot and raised his thumb as he spoke rapidly into a small rectangular microphone over his lips. A seaman hanging from a strap leaned forward and yelled into the pilot's face, motioning with a jerk of his head toward the boat below. The pilot shook his head and with two flicks of his forefinger pointed to Eliot and the horizon. The helicopter suddenly swung around, banking hard, and Eliot's head rolled to the side and he was looking down at the deck. He saw them waving up to him, five Haitians standing and supporting each other, passing a jug of water. Many others were crawling toward the water jugs, and even some of those on their backs were waving and smiling. The helicopter circled around again and slipped down, and Eliot saw Alphonse emerge from his box. Alphonse stood stiffly, face raised, and turned slowly on his bare feet, watching the helicopter circle. The helicopter circled again, and Alphonse swiveled on the deck, never taking his eyes off the helicopter, his arms limp at his sides, and when the helicopter circled a final time Alphonse slowly raised his arms. Eliot blinked and Alphonse collapsed on the deck and Eliot looked down at the crumpled form until his face was pulled around gently by the chin. A smiling medic looked down at Eliot. The medic stuck an I.V. into Eliot's arm and wet his face and dribbled cold water into his mouth from an eyedropper. Eliot closed his eyes and closed his stiff lips around the long plastic nipple. The helicopter leveled and shot low across the turquoise sea.

General Markman's
Last Stand

THE GENERAL'S PANTIES were too tight. He clawed at his
hip, tried to get his index finger under the biting silk band. "Son
of a bitch," whispered General Trevor V. Markman, United
States Marine Corps, as the elastic wedged his finger against his
flesh. Markman twisted his massive torso; his back cracked. He
released his finger; the red panties loosened. He swiveled his
hips before the full-length mirror on the back of the wooden
door to his base office. The bra Markman pulled with shaking
hands from the mailing envelope was of matching silk, and
strapless. He slid the hefty cups around his back and was strain-
ing to fasten it in front when a hook snapped off in his hand.
Markman grimaced and tossed the new bra across his Camp
Lejeune office. The cups hit the Venetian blinds and let two
sharp bursts of afternoon light into the shadows of the office.

The hairs on his balls crinkled in their silk pocket. He cocked his hip, threw back his head, and shoved out his jaw. With slit eyes, watching himself in the mirror, Markman ran his fingers down to the panties, back up across his scarred chest. He cradled his jaw in his crossed hands, dragged his fingers across his cheek down the sunburnt ridges of his neck, and groaned. The crunching, rhythmic sounds of a platoon running by at double time wove for a moment with the drumming of his heart, and then it was over and it was no good.

Markman opened his eyes wide and studied himself in the mirror. He was a huge, hairy man in silk panties; nothing more. He shook his head and walked closer to the mirror and scratched the silver bristle on his head until white flakes filled the air. He turned and stared at the backlog of requisition orders spread across his desk. Captain Loring knocked on the door. Markman held his hands up before the mirror. Another platoon ran by outside. A sergeant barking orders, his voice rasping. The skin on Markman's hands was cracking, ravaged. He balled his fist and winced. Loring knocked on the door again. Markman ran his fingers over his chest. It was muscular, rigid. He looked over at the soft cups of the broken bra under the window, at the phone, at the empty mailing envelope, at his watch. He walked to his small fridge, took out a plastic gallon of bottled water, poured the cooling water over his inflamed hands. Markman bent his head down and cascaded the water over his head. Captain Loring knocked again. Markman straightened and hurled the jug at the door.

Markman slipped into the lingerie department of the post exchange. He didn't expect to find anything worth a shit. A decade of catalog purchases had raised his standards: He knew, and quickly reaffirmed, that the Marine Corps didn't put *beaucoup* imagination into its lingerie. The air-conditioning was off in the PX and the Muzak martial. Markman fingered a combined bra-straitjacket; the silk was soft and comforting on the back of his burning hand. Markman fell into a trance of touch. A bovine enlisted wife passed by in the aisle, gazed vacantly at him. A couple of recon marines were taking turns punching each other in the gut at the far end of the toy aisle. A child knelt beside them aiming a plastic bazooka at Markman. He felt faint, and grabbed the chrome bar holding up a row of traditional-cut white rayon panties covered with the faint gold imprint of the Marine Corps's anchor-and-globe insignia.

Markman's life had become a microwave oven, cooking him slowly and invisibly from the inside out. As his retirement approached, his fevers had increased in frequency and intensity. Lingerie cooled him: like parachuting out into a cloud bank. But now, as he stood in the PX, Markman felt the last moisture within him boil off. He saw black dots swirl before his eyes, threw out his left hand to find the bar on the other side of the aisle, and felt something silken under his calloused palm. He twiddled it with his trigger finger, found the spacious cup, and thrust his fingers deep into the forgiving, erogenous interior. He plucked the bra off the rack and with one sudden and smooth motion stuffed it down his green camouflage utility trousers.

After he left the PX and stepped into the North Carolina sun, Markman paused to slip on a pair of aviator shades, silver and straight at the ear. The attack of vertigo had passed; he was again satisfactorily military. A private was weeding with an old bayonet along the side of the concrete walkway. He stabbed the bayonet in the lawn, jumped up, saluted, and said, "Good afternoon, General."

"At ease, Marine."

"Aye, aye, sir!"

The marine remained ramrod. Markman closed his eyes and tried to remember his destination. He pictured himself marching naked except for his boots in a rainstorm—arms out, head back, mouth open. The rain sizzled and evaporated when it touched his skin. Markman opened his eyes and discovered anew the frozen young marine, chin tucked violently back into his wattled neck.

"I said . . . at ease, Marine," said Markman.

The marine dropped his shoulder a few inches, but stood stiffly. Markman squinted at a vulture circling in a wobble beneath the cobweb of clouds.

"Squared away, Marine . . . for the Corps's Birthday Ball tonight?" Markman said, without taking his eyes off the bird.

"Yes, sir," said the private. "Sir?"

"Private?"

"Sir," he said. "I joined the Marine Corps because of you . . . permission to ask . . . is it true the general is retiring today, sir?"

"Private," said Markman. "In my time in this Marine Corps I have tried to impress the men under my command that they are free as Americans to ask me anything . . . and I am free as an American not to answer." Markman reappraised the marine, noted the peach fuzz on his face, and said, "I am retiring because I promised my better half thirty years ago tonight that I would spend no more than three decades serving with you fine men. No lie has ever crossed these lips headed in the direction of Beatrice Markman, and I do not intend to commence at this late date in our hitch. Understood?"

"Yes, sir," said the private.

A Harrier jet streaked low across the base. Markman raised his thumb in a salute, turned to watch as the jet twirled and bent upward into the clouds. When there was nothing left but a fading jet trail, Markman was still watching the sky, the private waiting at attention behind him.

"Carry on," said Markman suddenly, and he continued down the path and across the street to his car, where he was approached by two tall MPs. One raised his hand and said nervously, "General Markman ... sir ..."

Markman stopped, took off his shades, and squinted. The two MPs shifted from foot to foot.

"At ease, Marines," said Markman.

One of the MPs said to the air over Markman's head, "Sir, we had a report." The second MP nodded and continued, "Sir, a report from the PX. Is there something down your trousers, sir?"

Markman raised his chin, ground his molars together, and remembered the bra. Beatrice had sent her lingerie to him monthly for the three years he was a young officer in-country. Her bras, panties, and nighties were humped in his rucksack all over Vietnam. He shoved them down his shorts and swaddled his nuts in silk when he had a bad case of crotch rot and fell asleep in the bush with silk clenched in his fist, his wife's smell shoved under his nose, lulling him to sleep. When he was horny he wrapped a bra around his head like a gas mask and beat off into her nightie. Markman put the end of his shades in his mouth, sucked, and recalled grabbing the bra at the PX. He reached down his trousers and took out the bra, sniffed it once, and while handing it to the MP said, "You may not understand, son, but these things saved my life."

As Markman was driven past the depot station, a bus full of marines fresh from Parris Island was unloading, their shaved skulls catching the sun. The dispatcher crackled over the radio for a response to a 187 at the Lejeune's B-12 small-arms range.

"Sergeant?" said Markman. "187?"

"A gunshot wound, sir."

"Should you respond?"

"It's a call for the coroner, sir."

"Accident?"

"Negative, sir. Self-inflicted."

Markman rubbed his hands over his head and tried to understand why he had taken the bra.

"Sergeant," said Markman. "You mind if we stop at the Division CP?"

"General?"

"Seventeen hundred. Colors. I never miss it."

"No problem, sir."

Markman leaned forward in the military police car and handed a tape through the slat beneath the cage. He always kept a couple of John Philip Sousa tapes inside the side cargo pocket of his utility trousers.

"Would you play this tape for me, Sergeant?"

The MP looked in the rearview mirror at Markman.

"Did you steal the tape, sir? Because if you did, I would have to bag it as evidence."

"No, son, that's my tape. You're Gonzalez?"

"Yes, sir."

"Are you proud to be in the Corps?"

"Yes, sir," said Gonzalez. "*Semper Fidelis.*"

"Good man. Now put in that tape."

Markman was driven back to the CP to "Semper Fidelis," and after watching the flag lowered to evening colors over the PA, continued on to the Staff Judge Advocate office on Lejeune

Boulevard to "Stars and Stripes." The second MP sat in the passenger seat, refusing to look at Markman. When the trio arrived at the Staff Judge Advocate office, General Markman looked out at the low brick building and said softly, "Attack."

Major Rawlings saw the MPs come in on either side of General Markman. Rawlings put Markman on ice in a side room and told Lieutenant Barnwood to take a report, locked the MPs in his office, dropped the bra in a black evidence bag and slid it into his desk under some files, and buzzed General Bowles' office.

Lieutenant Barnwood looked at General Markman sitting before him and said in a southern drawl, "I heard about you when I was a boy, sir. My father was a master sergeant in Vietnam, and he told me some things."

General Markman said, "Your father was a good man, Lieutenant?"

"Yes, sir," said Lieutenant Barnwood. "I believe he always did his duty to his God, to his Country, and to his Corps."

"How'd he treat your mother?"

"General?"

"I said: 'How did he treat his wife?'"

"With due respect, sir."

"Your people Baptist?"

"Yes, sir," said Lieutenant Barnwood. "How'd you know?"

Markman leaned back in the swivel chair. He felt like there was a firefight going on around him and he had been stripped of his weapon.

"Sir?" said Barnwood. "I don't believe—"

"You have some questions for me, Lieutenant? I suggest you get on with it."

"Yes, General. You had some article on your person from the PX?"

Markman sliced the air with his hand and said, "Barnwood, I stole a bra."

"... Did you say you *stole*, sir?"

Markman stood and said, "I stole the bra, Barnwood."

Lieutenant Barnwood raised his pen and said, "Sir... sir... you *stole* the article?"

Markman put both hands on the desk and said, "I'm not communicating, Barnwood? I stole the bra, shoved it right down these here camouflage trousers." Markman stood up and exhibited his hand shoved down his trousers. Lieutenant Barnwood fell back into his chair and jumped to attention when he saw General Bowles entering the room. Markman looked over, his hand still down his trousers. Bowles shut the door slowly and pushed out his lower lip with his tongue. He touched the side of his nose tenderly with his finger and said, "Son, if you would excuse us two warriors, we apparently have a lot of catching up to do."

Lieutenant Barnwood shuffled together his papers, while General Bowles hawked over him. As the lieutenant reached for the handle to the door, Bowles grabbed him by the collar. "Lieutenant, you are to forget you were ever in a room today with General Markman, or I will shoot you myself. Do I make myself clear?"

"Yes, General," said the Lieutenant.

General Bowles put his hand on the lieutenant's cheek and turned his face toward him. "What I am saying, son, is that I don't even want you talking to your sweet Jesus about what you think you heard."

General Bowles' face pulled together into a fist.

"Understood, sir," said Lieutenant Barnwood, and Bowles shut the door after him.

General Bowles curled his upper lip, closed his black eyes.

He took out a cigar and pushed it between his lips, keeping his back to Markman.

"We're going to take this from ground zero, and work our way along slowly so a simple mind like mine can understand," said Bowles. "Now, am I correct in stating this is your final day as a marine on active duty before retirement?"

"That's right, Bowles."

"And so, on your last day in the Corps, you wander into the PX and perform an act of thievery on an article of women's undergarments? Tell me this is not our present situation."

"I stole the bra," said Markman.

General Bowles fixed his eyes on Markman. "Don't say that."

"It's a fact."

Bowles took two steps toward Markman, then paused and leaned over so their faces were only a few inches apart, and whispered, "Do I want the facts?" Bowles tore the cigar from his lips; he spun and threw it against the wall of the office. The action drained him, and Bowles scratched the flaking skin behind his ear and said without turning around, "I never liked you much, Markman." Bowles took the seat at the desk, rested his hands across his gut. "We have a problem here, yes we do."

Markman raised his chin in the air.

"You can't run through this. Not this one. Tomorrow, Rawlings will press formal charges against you. Best we can do is control the collateral damage." Bowles shook his bald head. "Once, we could have swept this shit under the rug. Faggots, dick-hating bitches, and pussy-eaters run this country now."

"I understand," said Markman.

"You understand," repeated Bowles slowly.

"I'll take the flak."

Bowles jumped out of his chair and screamed, "Don't you think I'd love you to choke on your own shit!" Bowles waved his arms wildly, as if trying to clear smoke. "First thing civilians are going to think is a decorated Marine Corps general is a... cocksucker!"

"I'm... not AC-DC, Bowles."

Bowles pressed out his palms repeatedly, as if trying to stop an oncoming car. "Stop right there, Markman. I don't want another fucking word."

Markman heard a howl of wind in his ears, felt shrapnel sear into his chest, saw the room blacken. There were sounds ahead, his men screaming his name, the ambush at Quang Tri. He wanted to press forward, but for the first time Markman was running away, the jungle slapping him in the face. "I took... it... for myself," he said.

"Say what?" said Bowles.

Markman turned and started running back to the rattling of the M-16s and Kalashnikovs. Sergeant Castillo ahead of him on the trail took a round in the forehead; Markman caught him before he hit the ground. Castillo's eyes greased over as he looked up, his brains falling like worms out the back of his skull. Markman fished in his rucksack and pulled out a pink nightie, tried to stuff the hole in Castillo's skull with the yard of silk.

"I took the bra for myself," repeated Markman.

"Did I hear you correct, Markman?" said Bowles. "Did you say you want to suck my dick?"

Bowles unbuttoned his fly and hung out his gray cock. Markman stood up. Bowles grabbed his service pistol from his side holster, moved closer, and pointed the gun at Markman's temple. "I'd rather shoot you right now than see you dishonor my Corps. I took care of one of you bastards in Nam, and I've got nothing against doing it again. If you were a man of honor, you'd do it yourself."

"I didn't want...," said General Markman.

"You're a faggot, Markman," said Bowles. "I kill faggots."

Bowles pressed the muzzle of the gun hard into Markman's temple.

"Shoot me," said Markman, suddenly reaching up and wrapping his hand around Bowles' gun hand and squeezing. When Bowles felt Markman working his thumb on top of his trigger finger, he cracked his elbow into Markman's face, the nasal bone crunching like a walnut.

Markman slumped into the chair.

Bowles prowled around the edge of the room, put the gun back in the holster at his waist, tucked his dick back and buttoned his fly, adjusted his web belt, kicked the toe of his black boot through the wall. He ran back to Markman, waggled his finger in his face, and said, "I'll promise you one thing right now. No way in hell are you going to hurt my Marine Corps. Do you understand me, you dick-sucking motherfucker? You're going out tonight looking one pussy-loving son of a bitch."

Markman was sitting in the bar in the Officers' Club, eavesdropping on a captain describing the gang bang of a high school girl in Washington. Markman pictured the three naked marines, cocks at attention, sitting on the other bed in the Holiday Inn, waiting their turn to flop on the girl. "The bitch was bleeding and still couldn't get enough dick," said the captain. "We all went around a second time."

"General Markman?"

Markman turned slowly from the bar.

"General Markman, what happened to your face?"

"General Bowles broke my nose."

Lieutenant Hardie laughed, showed his fine teeth.

"Sir, General Bowles told me I could find you here at the O Club."

General Markman turned back toward the leather-lined bar and picked up his empty glass of Jim Beam, placed it back on the bar, and waved to the bartender.

"General Bowles told you I was here?"

"Yes, sir," said Hardie. "He told me I was to remind you to leave the O Club at eighteen hundred sharp for your appointment. He said, and General Bowles made me memorize this, sir: 'If you truly love your Corps and are looking forward to your retirement with Beatrice, you won't miss your appointment at eighteen hundred hours in the parking lot outside the O Club.' Don't know what General Bowles means, sir, just passing the word."

Markman rapped his knuckles on the stool next to him.

"Have a drink with me, Hardie."

"I would be honored, General."

Markman stared at his reflection in the mirror behind the bar as his glass was refilled, and then drained it, pointed for another. The bartender looked at Hardie.

"Double shot of Jim Beam," said Hardie.

Markman took a sip from his glass and said, "You have a woman in your life, Hardie?"

"Yes, sir."

"Is she a keeper?"

"General?"

"Can I advise you, Hardie?

"Yes, sir. Anytime, sir."

"Marry her, Hardie. The Corps is hard on wives, so be good to her. If it wasn't for Beatrice, I wouldn't have come back from Vietnam."

"Sir, may I ask you a personal question?"

"I may not answer, Hardie."

"You really dove on a Viet Cong grenade?"

Markman looked away.

"You don't have to answer, sir."

"I saw it and fell on it, Hardie," said Markman. "If I'm not under fire, I'm not worth a shit."

"I can't believe that's true, sir."

"It is true, Lieutenant Hardie," said Markman. "I've no brain for staples and paper clips. I could take the objective in a firefight, and I could dive on a grenade. Those are limited talents in the real world."

"You wouldn't be a general if that was all."

"That is all," said Markman. "I'm General Markman because they liked the way my hair went white after the grenade. It was just dumb fucking luck it wasn't live. Woke up the next morning and Blake, my platoon sergeant, said, 'Lieutenant, your hair, it's gone white as snow.' Blake bought it that afternoon, took a chest wound for me. Stepped right in front of me. Couldn't get a medevac. Blake only had sixteen days and a wake-up. He was a good man and a good friend."

"Begging your pardon, sir. You're not a general for your hair."

Markman ran his hand over his head.

"Got more dandruff than hair," said Markman. "But you're right, Hardie. I'm a general because a lot of gooks are dead. My units always had the highest body counts. Wherever I went in Nam, gooks got transformed into fertilizer."

Hardie opened his mouth, but Markman raised his hand and said, "Until I shove off, don't say anything."

Markman had always told his men he expected them on time for their own funerals. He swiveled around and examined the wooden doors of the Officers Club, ripped back the Velcro cover, and checked his watch. Bowles had said to be in the parking lot at 1800. Markman slid off the stool, straightened

30

his camouflage blouse, snapped it downward from his thighs, and brushed the dandruff off his shoulders.

Hardie got off his stool and stood next to Markman.

"I'm heading out, General," said Hardie. "To prep for the Ball."

Markman nodded and headed for the door. From the corner of his eye, he saw Hardie motion to a number of officers standing down the bar. One of the officers had a white rat on his shoulder painted with the blood red letters USMC. Shot glasses in pyramids lined the bar, and the officers were singing:

> *From the halls of Montezuma*
> *To the shores of Tripoli;*
> *We fight our country's battles*
> *In the air, on land, and sea;*
> *First to fight for right and freedom,*
> *And to keep our honor clean;*
> *We are proud to claim the title of*
> *United States Marine.*

Markman put on his aviators as he stepped from the Officers Club, although the sun had been down for an hour and the trees across the parking lot had fused into a single dark shadow. He stood on the curb clenching and unclenching his hands.

Markman walked slowly to the center of the parking lot, and Hardie followed. General Bowles had ordered him to glue to the general and make sure he was in the parking lot on time but hadn't given him specifics—except to bring along as many young officers as possible. There were more than a dozen watching from under the awning outside the doors of the O Club.

Markman stopped with Hardie a few steps behind him. Markman looked up and down the parking lot, and then his head cocked. Hardie heard it, a rapid clicking, and then from behind a green van emerged a woman, hustling toward Markman, her breath coming in heaving gusts. Her blond hair was a wobbling pyramid, her large gold earrings glittered in the faint light, and her mouth quivered in a red circle of sputtering lips.

"You bastard, Markman!"

She swung her large black purse, caught Markman across the head. Hardie involuntarily stepped backwards and saw the general's head snap back, his sunglasses hang off an ear and fall to the ground. She must have a brick in there, Hardie thought. Markman did not raise his arms, and the woman dropped the bag and pummeled him across the face and chest. Markman stepped forward into the blows. "How dare you stand me up on my birthday! You promised me lingerie! Shit on you!" Markman looked down at the unknown woman slapping him.

"Christ," said Lieutenant Hardie.

Hardie took a tentative step toward Markman. From behind came the laughter of the group of officers who had followed them out of the O Club. One officer yelled out, "She's a grenade, General, you should dive on her!"

"General," said Lieutenant Hardie.

Hardie heard the laughing officers moving closer to the scene, heard the door to the O Club opening, and the other officers running toward the general. The woman had now gone limp in Markman's arms and was sobbing against his shoulder. The officers crowded around them in a tightening circle: clapping, whistling, high-fiving, and chanting, *"Markman, Markman, Markman . . ."*

Markman walked around his house turning on the humidifiers he had recently placed in every room. He sighed and went to the stairs. Markman stopped on each step and touched the family photos. Trevor, Jr. was at Hampshire College, studying theater; he wore a gold stud in his lower lip. Nicole was in her last year at the Georgetown School of Foreign Service. Blake was a plebe at West Point and had shaved her head to match the male plebes. The children were organizing a surprise retirement party for the weekend. Markman ran his fingers over the wedding photo of his wife Beatrice, the only daughter of Major General Kittridge. Markman had shipped out for his first tour in Vietnam the day after their wedding.

Markman came to the door of their bedroom. Beatrice was in a white gown laced with gold trim, sitting at her dressing table with the back of her dress open to him.

"Hello, Beatrice," Markman said from the doorway.

Beatrice turned her head, but said nothing when she saw her husband's bloody, swollen face.

"Beatrice," said Markman.

Beatrice put down her mascara.

"Go on, Trevor."

"I cannot cross this line . . . ," began Markman.

Beatrice remembered the last time she had heard such a formalized beginning: Markman had slept with a prostitute in Saigon after the grenade incident during his second tour in Vietnam. He wrote to Beatrice asking her forgiveness. She wrote Markman back a twenty-page letter that began, "Trevor, I would rather die than have you lie to me. . . ." Beatrice's brief first marriage had been with a sailor who slept with her bridesmaid Pauline Padgett during the wedding reception, took Beatrice's virginity later in the evening, gave her (and Pauline Padgett) gonorrhea, and then shipped out for a twelve-month tour on the U.S.S. *Tripoli*.

"Tell me, Trevor," said Beatrice.

"I cannot cross this line without telling you," said Markman.

"I have been having an affair. I broke it off this evening outside the Officers Club. There was a scene, people will be talking tonight at the Ball."

Beatrice put out her hand as if to stop a fall. Her dress fell off her shoulders, slipped down her thin arms to her waist. Her breasts were small, sagging, tear shaped. She closed her eyes. Markman walked into the room, took her by the shoulders.

"It was stupidity."

"But we make love almost every morning."

"We do," said Markman softly.

"And you're home every evening."

"I am."

"We don't even go out on the weekends anymore."

Beatrice shoved Markman away and pulled her dress up over her shoulders.

"I want a divorce, Markman," said Beatrice. "I don't know what's going on, but I know you're lying to me."

Markman went to the cellar and sat in the dark under his house. He listened to the water rushing through the pipes when a toilet flushed above. He unlocked a chest, undressed, and put on a frilly yellow bra and panties he had hidden away since Vietnam. In the dark, running his hands over the bra across his chest, he felt a comfort running through his veins. He put his camouflage uniform back on, went upstairs and took his dress blues into the bathroom, took off his camouflage uniform, shaved, and slowly, as if in a trance, put on his high-collared dress blues.

Markman held his cock in the head at the O Club, watching the piss splash over the pink deodorant bar on the bottom of the drain. The deodorant looked like pink ice and Markman wanted to hold it against his forehead. He was slapped on the shoulder, and his piss splattered against the porcelain wall of the urinal, sprinkling back on his hand.

"It must be tired," said Colonel Blair, looking over Markman's shoulder. Blair had been a lieutenant with Markman in Vietnam.

"Thought we were getting too old for that stuff," said Blair, waving his drink in the air. "But hell, you're a hero. How many girls you got, Markman? Two, three?" Markman buttoned his fly and Blair saluted and said, "It's too bad you're retiring. You've a cock to respect." Blair bent over and saluted Markman's crotch and dropped his drink. He pushed the broken glass around with his dress shoe and said, "Fuck it, let those bastards mop it up." Blair left the head and Markman walked over to wash his hands. He opened the faucet, backed away, and listened to the steady rush of water.

Markman walked out of the head, leaving the faucet running. A table of officers called to him, made pumping motions with their fists, and raised their wineglasses to him. Their wives laughed and clapped their hands. One officer stood up and called out, "You the man, General Markman! More I hear about you, the harder I get!" He repeated it three or four times with escalating emphasis on the word "*man*," and then sat down nodding to himself as if he had settled a pressing issue. Markman went back to his seat at the head table, and Beatrice turned away when he sat down.

Sally Prescott, wife of Colonel Prescott, leaned over and pressed her dry lips against his ear. She whispered, "Prescott has prostate problems, Markman, can't even get it up anymore." Markman turned his face and Sally Prescott nodded her small head and gave him an eager grin. The white powder on her nose was caked like phosphorus on a used flare canister. Sitting next to her Colonel Prescott looked blankly at the officers in the dining hall. Prescott was animated only when talking about his military stamp collection. He turned his head and blinked at Markman, the corners of his mouth cracking upward.

"Beatrice," said Markman, slipping his hand onto her thigh. She reached under the table, lifted it like a crane, and it dropped limp between their bodies.

Major Embrie was applauded when he said, "So with luck we'll get some trigger time in the coming year, grow the hair on the balls of some of you virgin lieutenants..." When he was done, he nodded to Markman as he made his way back to his chair. Someone threw their wineglass against the fireplace, and then there was a cascade of shattering crystal. Markman looked down the table, but none of the other senior officers raised their heads at the breaking glass.

"I wish," said Markman. "I sometimes wish I was a lush."

"What?" said Sally Prescott. "Did you say something?"

"Nothing," said Markman. "Talking to myself."

The civilian waitresses brought in trays of shot glasses, and toasts were made to the Corps, and to the wives, and the shot glasses were hurled against the fireplace. Markman had seen glasses thrown in bars off-base, but never at the Officers Club, and the Corps's Birthday Ball was usually particularly formal, at least this early in the evening.

"Beatrice," said Markman, touching her shoulder and wanting to discuss this with her. His wife shivered.

"I want the truth, Markman," said Beatrice, looking straight ahead over the sea of blue gentlemen. "Other than that—cease and desist. That's an order."

The gigantic white, red, and gold birthday cake was wheeled into the room, escorted by six marines, and the band played a slow, lugubrious version of "The Marines' Hymn." At first the officers were silent and at attention, and then they broke into cheers, a few of the new lieutenants throwing back their heads and bellowing the Marine Corps seal call of "OOhrah!" One young officer pounded on his table and cried out, "Markman! Markman! Markman!" The call was taken up by the other officers, and the standing, chanting soldiers smiled at Markman. The cry changed to "Speech! Speech!"

Another round of shot glasses was brought out, they too were thrown, and a lieutenant stood on his table and made a toast to the memory of General Lewis B. Puller until his legs were yanked out from under him and he went face down on the floor. When he stood, there was blood on his chest. He grinned and pulled a triangular shard of glass from the front of his dress blues, put it between his teeth, snapped it in half, spit out one half and balanced the other on the tip of his nose. The officers cheered and made him chug three shots in a row. When the officer on the table had downed the shots, he raised his fists over his head and waggled his knees as if he had just scored a touchdown. The room applauded, and he made another somber toast, little of which was comprehensible.

Colonel Prescott went to the podium, bent his tall frame, and said into the microphone, "General Markman, as we all know, is retiring tonight. I believe all of us have heard how he bravely he stood his ground in the face of a recent assault..." The marines hooted and Colonel Prescott smiled broadly and said, "General Markman, will you please talk to these good men!"

Markman had his eyes pressed shut. He was back at Quang Tri, there was a firefight ahead at the edge of the rice paddies. The marines screamed out his name.

"General Markman?"

Markman walked toward the firefight. He opened his eyes, and took a deep breath. Beatrice stared at her plate, her fading blond hair falling around her face in a curtain. He had dreamed of that hair mopping across his chest when he was humping through Nam; the memory of it had often kept his legs in motion long after all else was gone.

"General Markman?"

Markman pushed back his chair, felt it scrape across the wood floor. The roar in the auditorium rose and a few more glasses shattered in the fireplace. The glass-chewing marine was dancing in front of the head table. Colonel Prescott nodded at two officers and the marine was dragged away laughing maniacally; halfway out of the hall he vomited down the front of his dress blues and the officers applauded when he licked his lips. Prescott beckoned again to Markman, holding the place at the podium.

"Did I say he is the most humble marine in the Corps?" said Prescott, leaning down to the microphone as if it was miles away.

As Markman moved slowly to the podium, he saw a Viet Cong grenade rolling toward him, felt his body leap forward and stretch out in the air.

As he stood at the podium, Markman saw Beatrice walking toward the exit between the tables of cheering officers. He watched her retreating from him, reached up, and unclasped the stiff collar of his dress blues.

He saw the grenade under him now, saw it wobbling along the burned ground.

The marines hooted and howled, "Markman!"

Markman landed on the grenade. The breath was knocked from his chest in a broken gasp. He craned his neck around to look at his men, who stared back at him in horror from the elephant grass.

At the door to the banquet hall, Beatrice paused, and looked back as Markman popped the anodized brass buttons of his jacket. Markman dropped his arms to his side and shook his hairy, shrapnel-scarred shoulders, letting the jacket fall behind him to the floor.

Markman, never taking his eyes from his wife, slipped off his dress shoes and loosened his web belt with the raised Marine Corps insignia and dropped his blue trousers. He raised one bullet-scarred leg and climbed atop the head table in front of Major Learned's hyperventilating wife Agnes, and lowered his arms to his side.

The air in the hall froze; the fat on the plates congealed. There were sounds from the kitchen at first, but then these faded out as the silence spread like a nerve agent. The enlisted cooks silently slid from the kitchen and lined the back wall. The wind could be heard in the trees outside the glass doors at the far end of the hall. The candles flickered. There were footsteps across the floor in the room above.

One officer finally walked in front of the head table and without looking at Markman made his way to the exit. Another followed a few seconds later, and a third broke away from the iceberg of officers. Marines and wives silently floated from their tables and out of the hall. Not one looked up at the man on the table.

Markman never took his eyes off Beatrice.

As the marines left the room with their wives in an ebbing flood of blue, as the starched, uniformed backs turned on her husband, Beatrice Markman began to clap, gingerly at first, and then with determination.

Scar Vegas

THE COWBOYS cracked my ribs but they are taped firm. I am now in Vegas after frying across the Texas panhandle in July top down because the top was broke up good when I was thrown through outside Amarillo my first real stop after Galveston. I like the convertible top up myself and I like air-conditioning on full cold and the radio low. I do not like the sky night or day and keep my eyes on the yellow lines heading under the car when I am moving on. A pretty girl throws me the finger as I roll down the Strip. It's soft asphalt hot in Vegas.

The door to 1137 is cracked and I kick it open slow with my boot toe. The cowboy boots screw up my knees and they click with floating bone. The knees are wanting for oil or I am higher on the odometer than yesterday. Room 1137 is empty. I take off my shades and hang them slow in my shirt. I click my knees in the empty room and breath easy the air-conditioned air. No air-conditioning in the Galveston prison.

My sister in her wedding dress jumps from behind the door. She grabs my jewels. She whispers, "Ain't you surprised, Johnny?"

No. I ain't surprised. I ain't never surprised. This world ain't never sprung nothing on me. Some people get themselves hit by lightning and other strange things but that ain't me at all.

Her hold on my crotch is not too bad. My sister's name is Janey but everybody always calls her Fruit. We are the Loops. Someone sure as hell is Fruit if you are the Loops. Fruit is stunted but busty and hippy and blond as bleach and smells like peppermint. It's not candy but perfume. When Fruit was a girl she wore peppermint perfume and she still wears it to this very day here in this hotel in Vegas the day before her wedding.

Fruit says, "Say uncle."

She squeezes more and down I go to my knees. We Loops are stubborn people and she ought to of known I wasn't going to say what she said to say. Things generally happen without my two cents. All I got is the right to open and close my mouth when it strikes me and not a minute before.

Fruit tightens up her hand more. She squeezes once hard and I thud over on the carpet. She says, "I'm glad you came, Johnny."

The groom is at the door to room 1137 in a cut-off shirt and shorts. I figure it's the groom. He looks like a bull at a rodeo before the gate swings open. This groom is snorting at the gate and comes into the room as if zapped by an electric cattle prod. Fruit's froze. He yanks her up like he's yanking a flower out of the ground roots and all. He swings her in a circle hooting and hollering. She is smiling in a concerned way as she goes round and clips me with a heel in the eye. Fruit goes round and round in her wedding dress.

The groom is a semipro football player. The groom is #22, Breezy Bonaventure. He flings my sister Fruit. A shot put in a wedding dress. She rolls across the bed and is lost on the floor behind. Breezy looks at the bed. Where'd she go? He looks angry. Soon enough I see him forget her. A dog forgetting a stick. When I ask Fruit when I call from Austin why she is marrying she whispers because she is sick of waiting.

Breezy sticks his head in the little fridge and slaps the wall with his hand. His legs are the color of Ivory soap. He pulls out two beers and sticks them on either side of his hips under the elastic band of his team shorts and a third he unscrews in his teeth and flicks the top across the room. Fruit climbs up on the bed and hides her face in a pillow. Breezy doesn't know me from a hole in the wall and comes over scratching his chin looking me over and finally he says pointing his beer, "Who you?"

"He's my brother Johnny," says Fruit from the pillow.

"Hell no," says Breezy. "You never said nothing about a brother."

"I did so say," says Fruit.

Breezy leaves Room 1137. Fruit says, "What'd you say, Johnny?"

"I didn't say nothing," I says.

Nobody called me Johnny in prison everybody called me Loop.

My sister Fruit has never played the slots and I buy her a bucket of quarters. In prison I made about a quarter an hour and she has a bucket of long hours in her hand. Fruit skips down between the machines in her wedding dress.

I do not like to gamble and done Vegas too many times. I am not lucky. Some people are lucky. The big finger in the sky is pointed at them. The big finger in the sky never so much as took the time to poke me in the eye.

Fruit puts the bucket of quarters down next to a slot. Fruit's got the slot arm.

"Go on," I says. "Give her a good yank."

I click my knees and Fruit pulls all lemons.

Fruit is looking at me.

"What," I says.

"You cut your hair."

"Long time ago."

She is real quiet.

"You ain't never . . . ," she says.

"Ain't never what?"

"Called or nothing."

"I called," I says. "I called and I come."

"One call. Four years," she says. "You was calling for cash. You was in prison."

Fruit says nothing more. I am now thinking about prison in Galveston. Two years. In prison there was a cellmate name of Reginald. All the time he says he is looking at the sky at night. There ain't no sky. Nothing but the bottom of my bunk all covered with various stains. Reginald says once to me he's long ago given up on people. Says after you are done with people there ain't nothing left to do but wait for a sign.

Fruit takes the quarters to another slot. She goes off down the long line of slots and she puts quarters from her bucket in the buckets of all the old ladies smoking butts at the slot machines. None of them even see. Fruit stops at the end of the row of slots and climbs on a stool.

He is overboned. An old steer. His clothes are beat to shit

13

but ironed and his cowboy hat is low over his eyes and clean to new. His belt hangs low and his thumbs are hooked in his belt. He leans over Fruit in her wedding dress like a tree in a hurricane. He is grinning and rubbing his nose with his thumb. He pulls back and stands up and wrestles up his pants some and moves back in again and raises his hand to her hair.

He touches her bleached hair with that horse hand because he ain't got no choice. He strokes her bleached hair and Fruit spins around and tries to slap away his big hand. She says something and the Texan moves in to give her a kiss. Fruit tries to hit him where it counts with her knee. Her knee is driving like a piston but can't do much in all the cloth of her wedding dress. The Texan is holding on to her by the shoulders as if he doesn't know what to do next.

The Texan never knows what hits him but I know. Breezy Bonaventure's skull spears him in the spine flat out. The Texan slams into two slots and is on the floor, a sorry sack of skin and bones. Fruit is on the floor in a wad of wedding dress. It takes five security guards to pull Breezy off stomping the Texan. Breezy is foaming. The Texan is twitching. I ain't moved a muscle.

I don't want no trouble.

The hotel got it on videotape. Breezy sees these replays all the time as a football player. He asks for a copy. The manager says it isn't allowed however much he'd like to oblige. The manager has a lot of paint in his hair and his teeth are far too bright and he looks afraid like if things go down he's going down much worse. The office is a jungle with plants. Fruit has a big white brace on her neck.

We three look at him in his office.

44

"We are a family hotel," the manager says.

"Yeah," says Breezy. "Family."

"Things like this shouldn't happen to a bride," says the manager.

"No sir," I says. "They sure shouldn't."

"Not to as pretty a bride as this young lady," says the manager.

Breezy shows his teeth again. The manager stands up short behind his desk. What the manager does is lead us up to a door on the seventeenth floor and gives Fruit a key. We all stick our heads in when the door opens and take a look round. The room is three times bigger than the last room. Big enough to spin a car in doughnuts. The whole place is bright pink. I put on my shades. Breezy goes into the room and walks in a circle and says, "Got any beer?" The manager shows him this wall that opens and there are all the beers in the world. Fruit sits in a big pink chair. She rolls from side to side to look at the room on account of her neck.

"This is all for us?" she says.

"We service thousands of brides a year," says the manager.

"That right?" I says.

"We're a family hotel," says the manager. "A place you can tell your friends and neighbors about when they're planning a wedding or choosing a family destination."

"Sure," says Breezy. "Family."

We all look at the manager. The manager crawls out backward. I shut the door and get a beer and give one to Breezy. He shoots the cap across the room and it plinks off the window. There is another big Vegas hotel right across and I look out and see into a hundred rooms. Fruit slides off the chair and gets a bottle of champagne. Breezy pulls the cork. The foam goes down his arm. Fruit takes the bottle and pulls open the glass door and goes out on the porch.

"You really her brother?" says Breezy.

"Yes I am," I says. "I am."

Breezy chugs his beer and tosses the empty across the floor. He belches and rubs his foot. I leave him belching and go out on the porch.

"Fruit," I says, "how come you never tell this guy you got a brother?"

"You was in prison."

"So," I says. "Lot of people in prison. I'm your only family."

"So," she says.

The sky is white and sick with heat.

"Nice dress," I says.

"I made it," she says.

"How long you say you know this guy?"

"Three weeks."

"You make the dress in three weeks?"

"No," she says. "The dress was a year."

"Pretty."

Fruit spits and we watch it fall. It goes a long way before it hits the building. We don't say nothing but I spit and it goes farther down. Fruit spits and it goes farther yet. Fruit gets a kick out of this so I do it with her for a long time and we drink the champagne. When I go back inside Fruit stays on the porch.

Breezy has a grapefruit in each hand. Down at the end of the room he has lined up beers. He rolls the grapefruit across the pink carpet. A strike. He sets up the beers again. He goes back down the end and rolls another grapefruit and rolls a spare. There are six empty beers. I sit down on the couch and Breezy bowls. He throws a gutter ball into the bedroom. He takes another grapefruit from the basket on the marble table. He throws a strike.

My sister Fruit comes flying in from the porch. I turn my head to look at her. She says, "Some guy is jerking off over there."

Breezy catches his swing and turns to her. His nostrils twitch. Fruit points at the hotel across the way.

"He was standing in the window naked," she says. "He was looking over and waving his thing at me."

Breezy breaks for the porch. I go to the window. Fruit is next to me. Breezy is out on the porch pointing and screaming at the other hotel. I shut the door to the porch. Breezy takes off his shirt and waves it at the pervert. His face is blue.

"Can you see the guy, Fruit?"

"He's gone," says Fruit.

Breezy barrels back in the suite. He takes the basket of fruit and drop-kicks it. Breezy picks up a round pink lamp. He shatters it on the marble table and cuts his hand. He stops and looks stupid at the blood. He snorts. He chugs a beer. He lies face down on the couch. His hand hangs off the couch and is dripping blood slowly off his fingers on the pink carpet. Fruit and I sit and say nothing.

Breezy snores.

Breezy says Fruit is in heat. So I go down to the lobby that night when the Sarasota Panthers come to town. I go to greet the team as the brother of the bride. Soon as I am down there by the waterfall I see them. The whole team is standing silent around the lobby like cattle. A few of them turn their heads slowly from side to side. The waterfall goes right up the inside of the hotel twenty stories and after a while two of them start to throw a football through the waterfall. People sitting near the waterfall stand up and applaud.

He raises his hand and they stop throwing the football. He has a flattop crew cut. A cut that comes from standing up in the back of a fast truck under a low bridge. His nose is all broke up and he has two black eyes. His squint says you is nothing to him. I go to meet and greet but Crewcut stiff-arms me out of the way and herds the cattle to the elevators. The manager brings over a handful of keys. The manager don't know me now. The whole team tries to push into an elevator. There is a happy brawl. The second elevator comes and there is another happy brawl. I turn and there is another player pushing a shopping cart filled with beer across the lobby. He is the only one wearing his team jersey. He has black hair and a chipped tooth and sticks out his hand.

"Lucas Fairweather," he says. "Tight end."

"Johnny Loop," I says. "Dead end."

"Friend of Fruit's?"

"Brother of Fruit."

"Fruit's a nice girl."

His skin is slick and maybe he is Indian.

"Want a beer?" says Lucas. He points down at the shopping cart. I feel a case. It is cool. Way up at the top of the hotel the Sarasota Panthers are screaming. I put my cool hand on my forehead.

"You all right, bud?" Lucas says. "You don't look too hot."

Lucas pushes his shopping cart toward the waterfall and I hold on to the metal wire edge. The Sarasota Panthers are howling from the top of the hotel and I want to puke up my insides. I sit down on the edge of the waterfall and Lucas sits down. Lucas opens the beer and hands it to me. Big orange fish swim over to us when Lucas sticks his fingers in the water.

"Where you from?"

"Amarillo," I says. "Least that's the last stop."

Both of us look around the big hotel. People are going every which way. From the casino room I hear bells and whistles and see a red light flashing and people freeze and crane their necks to see who won the jackpot. It must be a big jackpot because people come unfroze and are getting sucked into the casino like there is a big magnet in there. One old lady gets knocked over in the rush and everyone is stepping right over her and she puts her hands over her head. I stick my fingers in the pond and the fish dart away.

"Shit," I says. "Truth is, I ain't never been lucky."

"Everybody got some luck."

"No. I ain't never been lucky. I can see it now clear."

"Another beer?"

"Uh-huh."

Lucas sticks his hand in the water and the fish come over.

"See?" I says. "You're lucky. The fish comes right to you."

"You stick your hand in," says Lucas. "They'll come right over to you."

The beer bottle is dropped from twenty stories up the hotel. There is not much of a splash in the pond and no one notices but the two of us sitting there. The water settles back and all the pieces of the beer bottle are winkling around on the blue bottom of the pond. The fish are long gone to the other side. The Sarasota Panthers are all howling up there at the top of the hotel.

"You're lucky that didn't hit you," says Lucas.

"Nope," I says. "That ain't luck."

"It could of hit you."

"Nope."

"Sure it could of," Lucas says. "You were lucky."

"Luck ain't something that don't happen," I says. "Lots of things don't happen. Luck is something that happens. When you been fingered out."

Lucas is taking off his shoes and socks. He pulls up his pants to his knees and steps over into the pond. He walks right out there in the pond. When he gets there he bends down and picks up the glass and piles it like plates in his other hand. He walks right back and steps over and walks right across the floor to the reception desk and he hands that glass to the girl. The marble floor is all wet footsteps. While I look the footsteps dry right up.

Lucas and I sit there and drink beers and talk about nothing. Lucas is getting cut from the team soon because he's lost his killer instinct. Lucas knows when he lost the instinct but don't want to talk about it and he don't want to talk about being cut from the team. So we look at the fish and drink beers.

The Sarasota Panthers bail out of the elevator. One has a case of beer under each arm. Breezy is in the center of them. Crewcut makes him chug beers. The Panthers behind Breezy keep looking up the inside of the hotel. I look up in time to see the football coming down from up near the glass roof. Breezy looks up and drops his beer and raises his arms as if to catch the ball. At the last second Crewcut gives Breezy a shove and the ball hits Breezy smack in the face. The ball bounces straight up in the air. Crewcut grabs it and hands it to Breezy who is pissed off then grinning like there is nothing better than to have a football dropped twenty stories onto his face. The laces leave a red scar across his cheek. Crewcut starts whooping over and over, "Pervert Hunt!" The Sarasota Panthers file out of the hotel after Crewcut. Lucas gets up and follows and I follow Lucas. In the heat outside the hotel I am dizzy. Prison was hot as hell and so is the desert. I splash some water from a fountain on my face and we go into the hotel across and back into the air-conditioning where I am better.

The Sarasota Panthers go right to the elevators and fight to fit into one and also the second. We go up in the third with a Panther.

"What floor?" say Lucas.

"Seventeen," says the Panther. "The pervert's on seventeen."

"What pervert?" says Lucas.

"Some guy pulling his pud checking out Fruit. Who's this asshole?"

The Panther thumbs toward me.

"My friend's the asshole," says Lucas. "You got a problem?"

"I ain't got a problem. That pervert's got a problem. Yanking his chain and the woman's in a wedding dress. That's who's got a problem. I ain't got a problem. That pervert's got a problem. We're his problem now. He's got to deal with us. We're going to clean up his act. We're going to polish the floor with his face."

On the seventeeth the team goes into a huddle. Lucas and I lean against the wall. Lucas rustles up two beers. The team is huddled for a while and they clap and break and half the team goes one way and the other half goes the other way. Lucas and I slump down against the wall of the hotel. Lucas clinks his beer to mine. It is too quiet down both ways of the hall.

Lucas pulls up his arm and shows me a tattoo on his arm.

"Kind of looks like a tiger," I says.

"A panther," says Lucas. "A Florida panther. Our team logo. Now I'm cut from the team I don't know what to do about it."

"Do about what?"

"The tattoo."

"Why you got to do something? Lots of people got tattoos from things they don't do no more. Says you were once part of something."

Crewcut sticks his head around the corner and pulls it back. They are all sneaking around the floor. One tiptoes by and leaves a case of beer near us at the elevator.

We both drain our beers. Lucas keeps shaking his head. I go and get a couple more beers. We both have our legs straight out in the hall and Lucas is flopped half over. If someone came out of the elevator they might of thought we were gunned down. Nobody came through the hall and there was nothing but the sound of the air conditioner. A low hum.

"You hear the air conditioner, Lucas?"

Lucas listens and shakes his head.

"You ever think you ain't part of it all?"

"Part of what, Johnny?"

"The score," I says. "People is making a killing all around you and you have less than nothing to do with it. They don't even see you. Sometimes it makes me sick."

"I don't know, Johnny."

"I do know," I says. "I do know."

"You know what?"

"I don't know," I says.

"Sure you do, Johnny. You know."

"I don't know if I know," I says. "But I know they don't know me. That's all I know for sure."

Lucas is flat on the floor now. I put a beer in his hand and says, "Thanks for calling me Johnny."

I sit back with my head against the wall and sip the beer. We sit there for some time and I hear a ruckus down the hall. The sound keeps getting bigger and soon enough they come around the corner. The whole team. Under Crewcut's arm is a worm of a man. A skinny bald guy in a dirty muscle undershirt and boxers. He has about three gray hairs left on his head and looks about three feet long. Crewcut drops him on the floor and puts his boot on him. He squirms around like a worm but Crewcut pushes down on his ribs with his foot.

"The pervert?" I says.

"Yeah," says Crewcut. "What's it to you?"

Someone says, "He's a pal of Fairweather's."

Lucas pulls up to a sitting position.

"Are you sure it's him?" I says.

"Tissues spread all over the floor," says Crewcut. "He's been spanking all right."

"At least he's neat," I says. "Using tissues."

All the Sarasota Panthers are looking down at the worm on the ground. I says to the worm, "What's your name?"

The worm on the floor looks at me and says, "Ray Candleman."

"You waving your little thing at a bride?"

"No," Candleman says. "No bride."

"Hell," says Crewcut. "This is the pervert. Got a clear view of Fruit. We could see her from his room."

"How'd you get in his room?"

"We knocked."

Crewcut scoops up Ray Candleman and goes into the stairwell. The Sarasota Panthers follow. I get Lucas up and we follow the team up a few levels to the roof. It's just about dark. The roof is all gravel and tar. The Strip is lit bright and it looks like a carnival. There are a couple of broken chairs. Ray Candleman is bouncing like a sack of meal on Crewcut's shoulder. He looks happy and I figure he's gone round the bend. Crewcut drops him on the ground near the far edge of the roof. He kicks him and Candleman gets to his feet. He is wearing yellow socks up his skinny shanks.

Crewcut says to him, "Jump, you piece of crud."

The team circles. Candleman looks behind him and down twenty stories. Candleman smiles. A slow, stupid smile. A smile as if these is all his pals. A smile as if he's never had this many buddies. A smile as if he's ready to jump if it will make all these buddies stand around and talk up Ray Candleman some more.

Lucas pulls on my sleeve and says, "Let's go play the slots. I don't want to see this."

We go down to the casino and Lucas goes in to play the slots and I go to the bar. I see her looking over. She is dressed all in shiny spangles like her dress is made of a million little spoons. She keeps looking and I look behind me to see if maybe she is looking at someone else. There is nobody behind me. She is still looking and I point to my chest and she nods and I just about fall off my stool. I figure she must be a whore and try and settle down but she doesn't look like a whore somehow so I can't settle down. Her eyebrows make her look surprised and her lips are open just a crack. She comes over sweet as pie and after a drink I ask her and she isn't a whore she's a schoolteacher from Iowa just trying to get over a divorce with some of her girlfriends. She tells me she stays away from the slots because she isn't lucky and I say I know just how you feel no doubt about it. She tells me she grew up on a farm. She is ten times better looking than any woman who ever looked at me twice in my entire life.

Ray Candleman is naked on the floor of the hotel room and curled up on his side with his knees to his scrawny chest. There is no one else in the room but me and Ray Candleman. I kick him soft with the toe of my boot because I am thinking he maybe is dead. I am thinking he is dead but there is no blood or bruises. He is stiff under my toe and heavy. I kick him hard and his back rolls forward some and flops right back again. Now I think he is dead. I kick him hard again in the back. Now I am sure he is dead.

"You bastard, Ray," I says. "Don't you be dead."

I bend over and put my hand on his shoulder. The skin is hot as hell. His right eyebrow pops up and one eye flies open. It opens wide and Ray Candleman lays on me a slow wink like we are the best of buddies.

"Johnny?" someone says. "Johnny?"

"Who's there?" I says.

"Johnny Loop."

Someone is talking to me and saying my name but I can't see them and it is pissing me off.

"Johnny? Johnny?"

Sure enough I wake up from a dream. The whole Ray Candleman dead on the floor thing was a dream. I am on my side and there is Lucas Fairweather his face stuck in mine.

"Johnny?"

"What?"

"Johnny?"

I hear someone go, "He's conscious?"

Lucas blows his bad breath in my face again. I try and sit up but they push me back down. I struggle and swing my arm and hear one holler but there is such a pain in my back that it drops me back down.

"Damn," I says. "I been stabbed."

"Johnny," says Lucas. "You're in the hospital."

Lucas moves out of the way and I see a tall doctor. His face is all mouth. His mouth says, "You've had a nephrectomy, Mr. Loop. You're stable now."

"Say again?"

The doctor shakes his head and scratches his nose.

"Your right kidney, Mr. Loop," he says.

"What about it?"

"It's gone," he says. "It's been surgically removed."

"What the hell are you talking about?"

The doctor is shaking his head again.

"It's true, Johnny," says Lucas. "That thing's long gone."

I pull myself up even though it hurts like hell and says to the Doc, "Well how about you put it right back in where you found it? I got to get on to my sister's wedding."

Lucas says, "The wedding was yesterday, Johnny. You never showed up. Fruit thought you skipped town. Everybody's gone."

"Don't screw with me."

"I found you in the bar," says Lucas. "You were having a beer but you were all messed up. You said your back hurt and I took a look and brought you here."

All this time my hand is checking out this bandage on my back from my hip up to my ribs.

"He was having a beer?" says the Doc. "That's amazing. That's really amazing. He must have an amazing constitution."

"What's that mean?"

"It means you're tough," says Lucas.

The Doc looks at me for a long while and says nothing. He pulls out his pen as if to poke me but turns and jabs over and over at an X ray on the wall.

"You can see it here," says the Doc. "See the clips on the aorta at the renal junction? The clips on the minor arteries? This zipper here is where they stapled you up, Mr. Loop. A very neat job. I've seen them botch it. Can you see your other kidney here? You'll be able to live off that kidney, Mr. Loop."

"Married," I says. "I was going to get married. That's the last thing I remember. She was from Iowa."

The Doc put his pen slowly back in his pocket. "It's not as uncommon as you might suppose, Mr. Loop. I've seen three cases this year. On the black market your kidney might be worth a hundred thousand or more. Some people are desperate."

"No kidding," I says. "A hundred thousand?"

"Consider yourself lucky to be alive, Mr. Loop," says the Doc. "They might have taken both kidneys."

"They," I says quietly.

"Mr. Loop? Did you say something?"

"How many people come to Vegas in a year?" I says. "You know?"

"I don't know," says the Doc. "Millions."

"Millions?"

"Must be," says the Doc. "Why do you ask?"

"And you've only seen two others like me this year."

"Three."

"Three others?"

"No," says the Doc. "A total of three. Maybe two last year. Why?"

"Nothing," I says.

The doctor's beeper goes off and off he goes. Lucas looks at the clock and says, "Hey, Johnny. You're going to be OK."

"Lucas?" I says. "You hear that?"

"Hear what?"

"You hear him say how much that kidney of mine is worth to them?"

"I heard it."

"Would you of ever thought it?"

"Not me, Johnny," says Lucas. "Nothing in my body ever be worth that much."

"Lucas?"

"Johnny?"

"You want to see the scar?"

"I've already seen it."

"Is it something?"

"It's something all right."

Lucas walks alongside the bed later when I am rolled to a room and then he has to go back to Sarasota. He shakes my hand and is gone like he was never there. Out the window of the hospital I see all the colored lights of Vegas. Every light is someone throwing the dice or pulling the slot or getting hit at the blackjack table. Late that night I ring for the nurse and ask her to bring me a mirror. She gives it to me and turns and is leaving the room before I even have a grip. I get the bandages in hand and with a couple of good yanks pull the whole taped mess down.

In the mirror I see it looks like a long angry yellowish mouth with silver braces. It looks like a greasy mouth that might open and my ugly insides might vomit out all over the floor. I touch the metal zipper holding it all back with the tip of my finger. It will scar bad.

Until I fall asleep I imagine over and over them fingering me, Johnny Loop, out of all the crowds of nobodies and losers.

Unapproved Minutes of the Carthage, Vermont, Zoning Board of Adjustment

(As recorded by Town Secretary Betty Bradley)

CHAIRMAN HARRY GOMES opened the hearing at 7:40 P.M. in the Carthage Central School cafeteria noting that Zoning Board of Adjustment member Gloria Mack would be late as her husband, Homer, was down with postoperative pain from his recent surgery for appendicitis and son Mike's hockey game had gone into overtime and she was the only one left to do the evening milking. All other members of the Zoning Board of Adjustment excepting Brewster Hutchins informally agreed after discussion to sign a get-well card for Homer.

The purpose of this emergency meeting of the board was the appeal by the Montpelier-based radio broadcaster WIKD of Carthage's Zoning Administrator Neil Cato's recent Notice of Violation re WIKD's broadcast facility (250-foot communications tower), which is located on Mease Mountain behind the

Carthage Central School on property leased from Elaine and Moe Mease. The applicant (WIKD) is also requesting a stay of enforcement of the Notice of Violation.

Maryann Gingus interrupted the meeting to voice her opinion that the WIKD radio tower should be "blown the heck up" and displayed a large photo of her little angel Stacey, who is in Boston Children's Hospital awaiting a bone marrow transplant for acute myelocytic leukemia. Chairman Gomes asked her to please step down off the table lest she fall and break a leg and to wait for her turn to speak during the coming period of public comment, and order was restored.

Chairman Gomes explained the format of the meeting, which would be somewhat different than usual because it is expected to be a long process due to the large numbers of lawyers present representing WIKD, as well as the large number of citizens of the Town of Carthage present. Chairman Gomes asked that the lawyers for WIKD introduce themselves. Matthew Baines, attorney for WIKD, responded and introduced his co-counsels, John Messinger, Leslie Udell, and Milton Harms of New York, New York. Peter Simmons introduced himself as the real estate manager for Nynex mobile phones, an interested party with the Mease Mountain radio tower, and introduced the attorneys for Nynex Mobile, including John Harvey, Sam Samuelson, and Phil Tyson, all of Harvey and Blythe of Boston, Massachusetts.

Attorney for WIKD Matthew Baines also introduced Guy Barrad of the California Institute of Technology as a technical representative for WIKD and Nynex. Attorney Baines noted that expert Barrad was being put up at WIKD's cost and hoped that the proceedings could be completed expeditiously, as there was great expense involved in the housing and transport of such an out-of-state technical expert from across the country.

This secretary was passed the circulating photo of Maryann Gingus's daughter Stacey, who is in Boston Children's Hospital with acute leukemia. Stacey Gingus is a friend of this secretary's daughter Annie, as they both attend the third grade at the Carthage Central School, which is right next to this WIKD radio tower.

There was no lawyer representing those numerous Carthage residents present (numbering by this secretary's count more than 250 of our 852 citizens) and concerned about the potential radiation from the radio tower, but Brad Miller agreed to act as a temporary spokesperson in lieu of Maryann Gingus, the original spokesperson, who was not responding to questions from the chairman and would not lift her head from the table.

Attorney Baines of WIKD asked if tables and chairs might be found for the three standing lawyers, and Chairman Gomes supplied the only available chairs and tables, taken from the third-grade classroom of Stacey Gingus, who was sleeping over at the house of this secretary when she vomited and was run home at three in the morning and was seen later that morning by Dr. Skip Hadley at the Carthage Health Clinic and rushed to Boston for a bone marrow transplant for which she is still waiting, brave little thing. Chairman Gomes asked the lawyers sitting at the third graders' desks if they were comfortable and Matthew Baines, speaking as the representative for WIKD and interested corporate parties such as Nynex Mobile, affirmed they were fine.

As there was the possibility of a court proceeding following the possible rejection of the WIKD appeal by the Zoning Board of Adjustment, Chairman Gomes described the necessity of defining at this stage "interested party status" concerning the offending WIKD communications tower. There was a move by the lawyers for WIKD and Nynex to limit "interested party status" (those residents who could make an appeal to the Carthage Zoning Board concerning the tower) to those residents already on their records as claiming interference from the tower. After much discussion, Chairman Gomes stated that any citizen of the Town of Carthage would be accorded "party status," as surely, with its present (since Rocktober) 50,000-watt signal, which could be picked up in Canada, WIKD affected all Carthage residents. There were numerous objections to this from the lawyers for WIKD and Nynex, who jumped up and requested data from federal agencies and the definitions of "affected" and "resident."

It was settled by Chairman Gomes, proceeding with the issue of "interested parties," that at the very least those town residents at tonight's meeting were "interested," and each town resident present was requested to step forward and give his or her address. There were objections from WIKD's attorney Baines, who asked for the Carthage town directory and was unable to find Robert Adam's name listed at Old Hollow Road and it was clear this was going to be a time-consuming process. Maryann Gingus was helped from the cafeteria by Cy Hammond and Zoning Board Administrator Neil Cato. Order was restored, and Chairman Gomes requested a pitcher of water for his voice.

Zoning Administrator Neil Cato returned and stated Maryann Gingus was hyperventilating on the picnic table near the children's jungle gym but that Dr. Hadley from the Carthage Health Center was with her and she vowed to return, which was applauded by the majority of Carthage citizens present.

Chairman Gomes requested that Planning and Zoning Administrator Neil Cato outline the context within which his investigation and eventual decision was made to issue the Notice of Violation to WIKD concerning its radio tower. Zoning

Administrator Cato said he had prepared written notes which he would refer to. He read from the first page. He noted there were many areas in which the issue was very technical, but that technical credentials are not necessary to determine whether or not a zoning violation exists, to which WIKD attorney Baines objected along with three other attorneys before being overruled by Chairman Gomes, who requested that the lawyers remain seated, although some complained the small children's seats hurt their posteriors. Zoning Administrator Cato continued and stated the central question was whether the facts and circumstances as they currently exist conform to the representations, understandings, and conditions made at the time the zoning approval was granted six years earlier to the previous Carthage zoning administrator, Butch Calais. Stella Johnson interrupted and stated Butch Calais, God Rest His Soul, was a good man but never too bright a bulb after the accident on Upper Quaker Road.

Zoning Administrator Neil Cato continued and stated that he would like to make clear that the leukemia of the child Stacey Gingus (who resided on Mease Hill Road, six hundred yards due northeast of the 50,000-watt radio tower) was not in any way related to his issuing of a notice of zoning violation to WIKD, nor should anything be read into his recent painful divorce proceedings and the concurrent divorce proceedings of Maryann Gingus. Order was restored, and Chairman Gomes requested Zoning Administrator Cato to please refrain from parenthetical personal comments and get a grip on himself and present his case, even though Chairman Gomes knew that all Carthage citizens were aware of the touch-and-go medical situation with Stacey Gingus, who played soccer with his own daughter Emily, and that the board's prayers were with Stacey and the Gingus family. Mel Tormland asked whether the Zoning

Board of Adjustment might officially say a prayer for the little girl, who was catching frogs in his drainage ditch two days before she was stricken, and Brewster Hutchins of the Zoning Board wondered if this might be a violation of church and state. Attorney Baines, representing WIKD, stated that it probably was a church/state violation, but the board voted eight to one and the prayers were said for the child as her photo was silently held aloft by this secretary's nephew Eric Broyard, a classmate of Stacey Gingus' in the third grade at the Carthage Central School.

Zoning Administrator Cato continued with the reasons for his notice of violation issued to WIKD for its radio tower. He stated that since June 1—the date Stacey Gingus was helicoptered to Boston for treatment—he had been deluged with over seventy-two complaints from local residents concerning "interference" from the 50,000-watt radio tower. Zoning Administrator Cato said he determined that Carthage residents were experiencing interference from the Mease Mountain WIKD tower and that he had witnessed these problems firsthand. Attorney Baines for WIKD interrupted to ask if this interference was the "case of the singing toothbrush" and was told to retake his "damn" seat by Chairman Gomes to applause from many Carthage citizens. Chairman Gomes apologized to attorney Matthew Baines of WIKD for the expletive, and the apology was accepted.

Zoning Administrator Cato continued, and circulated copies of letters sent to his office concerning the WIKD tower as well as letters to Hank Cane of the District Environmental Commission and a letter from Maryann Gingus formally appealing the WIKD tower's zoning permit. Zoning Administrator Cato denied to Attorney Baines of WIKD that he coached Maryann Gingus and other town residents at a potluck meal at the home of this secretary as to the only possible legal avenues to get the CANCER TOWER torn down. Zoning Administrator Cato also denied he told any citizens of the Town of Carthage to write in their letters that they were picking up Led Zeppelin through their electric toothbrushes and other home appliances. Attorney Baines for WIKD questioned why so many residents referred to Led Zeppelin coming through their home appliances in their letters to the WIKD station manager when it would be shown that WIKD no longer played Led Zeppelin but a wide range of alternative music following a recent format change. Chairman Gomes was able to regain control of the meeting by stating he was a fan of Led Zeppelin and making the parenthetical personal comment that WIKD station manager Phil Sacks would have been better staying far away from "alternative whiners."

Zoning Administrator Cato stated that he wrote to WIKD station manager Sacks on November 15, informing him that he had an obligation to open an investigation into the town residents' appliance-interference complaints and that he had visited the Gingus farm on June 12 and this secretary's home on June 13. Cato described that he could hear WIKD over the telephone at both homes, and at the Gingus residence through the toaster and the electric toothbrush when it was placed in his mouth and activated. The oral cavity, Cato noted, seemed to amplify the music, particularly in the presence of saliva. The experience was not unlike having an interior Walkman, and it would not have been a painful experience except that he was a fan of bluegrass music and rock-and-roll made his teeth ache. Zoning Administrator Cato stated that he also visited the Methodist church, where WIKD was coming in over the headsets used by the hearing impaired and could be heard in the background of the public-address system. Zoning Administrator Cato said that sitting in the back pew he could clearly identify the Rolling Stones' "Honky Tonk Woman" during a mock sermon by Reverend Harmon. Attorney Baines of WIKD objected but, after consultation with WIKD station manager Sacks, stated that despite the new Alternative format, it was possible that "Honky Tonk Woman" might have been heard on WIKD, as it was a hook to get the baby boomers turned on to the new Alternative songs and was a worthy classic in its own right by any standard.

After some discussion of what constituted "classic rock," Administrator Cato continued that based on his own observation and a questionnaire distributed to the citizens of the Town of Carthage, it was not a matter of dispute that the tower was causing interference, and thus he issued the notice of violation to WIKD for its tower.

Maryann Gingus returned to the room at this point and stated she was ready to make a statement. There was some discussion from the WIKD lawyers, as this was not the time for public comment, and Chairman Gomes thanked WIKD for allowing her to speak at this time, as she wanted to return to Boston to be at Stacey's bedside.

Maryann Gingus stated that she was not here to point the finger at anyone for her always-healthy little girl Stacey's being so sick with leukemia in a Boston hospital. She passed out a WANTED FOR MURDER: WIKD poster she had posted around town and stapled to Carthage telephone poles and stated this was not her work. Chairman Gomes thanked her for her disavowal of this activity and asked her to continue with her testimony. Maryann Gingus continued and said she had noticed some problems in her home when the power on the WIKD radio tower was raised in October to 50,000 watts, such as rock-and-roll coming from her wall outlets and toaster, but that she was not the sort of person to make a fuss and believed in being a good neighbor but that this whole experience had changed her and she was no longer afraid. She said this had taught her a lot of what she was capable of, and not just as a woman and a mother. She said she had done some research which she would like to enter into the record. She said there have been few scientific studies on the safety of the ordinary radio frequencies invisible in the air all around us but that a study by Prausnitz and Susskind showed that exposure to radio frequencies for only 4.5 minutes per day produced leukemia or lymphoma in over a third of the mice tested as well as a four-fold increase in testicular atrophy. Brewster Hutchins of the Zoning Board asked for copies of the study by Prausnitz and Susskind for the board, and these were supplied to the board by Maryann Gingus.

Attorney Baines for WIKD protested that this medical evidence was not only unsubstantiated but irrelevant to the case at hand, which deals strictly with the WIKD radio tower's presumed interference with home appliances—the so-called singing electric toothbrush—and that the chairman should not allow this testimony in the record. Chairman Gomes instructed this secretary to disregard and strike from the record the above medical testimony. Maryann Gingus threw her remaining wanted posters at Attorney Baines of WIKD and order was restored with numerous ejections from the cafeteria. Chairman Gomes asked Reg Barlow to call Sheriff Toohey and asked Maryann Gingus if she could continue, and she did so and asked that her personal relationship with Zoning Administrator Neil Cato—which she said was probably public knowledge—not result in her being prejudiced against by the Zoning Board of Adjustment, many of whom she knew were deer-hunting buddies of her husband, Arnold, who was not so innocent himself re that trip to Montreal in April. Kate Cato, wife of Zoning Administrator Cato, was walked from the cafeteria by Randolph Wells and order was restored.

Attorney Baines for WIKD asked if the chairman was going to allow this irrelevant medical testimony to continue, and Chairman Gomes asked attorney Baines if he wanted a woman whose beautiful nine-year-old girl was dying of leukemia to be forcibly restrained from speaking by the members of the Zoning Board of Adjustment with a muzzle. Maryann Gingus protested the use of the word "dying," and Chairman Gomes apologized, and order was restored.

Maryann Gingus agreed to step down after passing out an informational folder. Although attorney Baines petitioned the chairman to proceed, he and the other members of the board took a brief recess to look at Maryann Gingus's scientific material. In her material was an article from a newsletter called *Microwave News* about a Mr. K, who worked on radio towers for fifteen years and died at age forty-five, having lost all sight, memory, speech, and motor coordination. Lawyers for Mr. K had introduced studies showing that monkeys exposed to radio waves developed neurofibrillary tangles, a classic sign of Alzheimer's disease. Chairman Gomes's own father, Leicester, suffered from Alzheimer's disease and hadn't spoken in years, and when the meeting resumed Chairman Gomes asked if there was any more information about Mr. K. Maryann Gingus stated she would try to find out more information concerning Mr. K and in continuing her testimony stated that evidence also showed radio waves can also affect pacemakers, defibrillators, and powered wheelchairs.

Zack Blessman interrupted to ask if it was true about the powered wheelchairs, and Maryann Gingus said her literature stated that power surges causing the chairs to lurch forward have been known to occur. Zack Blessman's grandfather Ellery Blessman had fallen in his wheelchair down the stairs of the family farmhouse on Sugar Hill Road in November and broken his neck.

Attorney Baines of WIKD approached the board and noted that the hour was growing late and that WIKD had not yet been allowed to make its case and be heard by the board and the citizens of Carthage. Chairman Gomes allowed attorney Baines to present his testimony, and attorney Baines stated that WIKD's expensive outside expert from California would now address the fundamental question of the evening, that of radio interference with home appliances, if this was amenable to the Zoning Board.

Chairman Gomes gave his assent to this while stating the Zoning Board of Adjustment regretted not being in a position to play God with regard to the medical issues. Reverend Harmon stated that he for one was not afraid to play God, if testimony from Him was required to exorcise the rock-and-roll musicians from the Methodist church. Old Leicester Gomes, who suffered from Alzheimer's disease and hadn't spoken in many years, stood at this point and stated repeatedly, "What if God was one of us?" It was determined that these remarks were lyrics from the Alternative singer Joan Osborne, picked up through Leicester Gomes's new hearing aid. The hearing aid was removed by Jenny Gomes, wife of Chairman Gomes, and the meeting resumed.

Guy Barrad of the California Institute of Technology was sworn in. Attorney Baines of WIKD asked if he might ask leading questions of his expert witness, as if this was a court of law, because Barrad seemed to be unable to speak and just kept staring at the elder Mr. Gomes. Attorney Baines asked if Barrad had prepared a technical report on the WIKD-radio-tower-interference question, and outside expert Barrad finally said that yes he had done so. Attorney Baines asked if he had copies of this report, and Barrad refused to respond, though the reports were clearly in his hand. Attorney Baines tried to remove the copies of the report from the hands of the expert witness but was unable to remove them and asked that the witness be allowed to step down, but Chairman Gomes said a lot of expense had gone into bringing him all the way across the country to the Town of Carthage and it would be throwing away good money not to let the man speak his piece to the Zoning Board.

Chairman Gomes asked expert Barrad if he had anything to say to the Zoning Board, and Barrad stated that attorneys for WIKD had not paid him the final third of his payment and had also refused to pay for his stay at Horse and Feathers B & B in Carthage but had booked him into "a smelly old converted barn," i.e., Rudy's Motel in West Carthage. Chairman Gomes acknowledged that this might cause consternation, and Rudy Smith interrupted to ask what exactly was meant by this remark. Chairman Gomes apologized to Rudy Smith and asked expert Barrad if he would like to continue and comment on the interference questions.

Barrad said he had visited the area of the WIKD radio tower one day earlier and used a high-quality portable receiver, a General Electric Superadio, and a calibrated spectrum analyzer (the Tektronix 2712) and had experienced considerable front-end overload. He added that this was a very unusual siting for a high-powered station tower and that he was not surprised that there would be ongoing interference problems. Most older radio towers achieve their geographic coverage by locating on remote mountaintop sites, where the height of the tower allows for reduced overall power. Due to most of these mountaintop sites being already in use, more towers were now being placed at less than optimum height and near residential areas. As the WIKD tower in Carthage was situated on what amounted to no more than a cow hill, it had to use significantly greater power to achieve its 50,000 watts. That, plus the unusual closeness to the residential community, clearly accounted for the appliance interference. Moe Mease, owner of Mease Mountain, stated that for the record the communications tower was situated on a MOUNTAIN and that he didn't know what exactly was meant by a COW HILL but he hadn't ever seen a cow standing up there and that the U.S. Geological Survey considered his land a MOUNTAIN by a good half dozen feet, which was good enough for him. He stated further that he bet it was good enough for the rest of the citizens of Carthage too. Chairman Gomes refused to put the issue to a voice vote of the citizens present, and asked that the meeting resume.

Attorney Baines of WIKD interrupted to point out that the testimony from expert Barrad did not reflect what Barrad had written in his report, of which he now held a copy, and asked that the verbal testimony be stricken from the record and the written record be entered as evidence. Chairman Gomes stated that expert Barrad from California was sworn in and thus his verbal testimony was valid. Chairman Gomes asked Barrad if he was sworn in when he wrote the report, and Barrad said that at the time he wrote the report he was not sworn in. Chairman Gomes told expert Barrad to proceed at his leisure.

Witness Barrad noted that his original written report stated only that WIKD was in compliance with FCC rules and that the interference problems were probably with the consumer devices such as faulty electric toothbrushes or toasters but that he now disagreed with this, as the problem would clearly go away if WIKD was switched off.

Attorney Baines of WIKD interrupted to ask if expert Barrad should not be getting back to California. Barrad stated that he was willing to stick around and stated that he would also like to comment on the health aspects of the tower—to wit, that there exists no federal standard or determination of adverse nonthermal effects of nonionizing radiation from radio waves and that the present recommended levels are being widely questioned. Barrad concluded by noting that waiting for the federal government was a bad gamble, and he cited all the studies linking smoking to cancer, about which the government did nothing. He stated that it was his belief that, with all the microwave towers going up for mobile phones, the national health was at risk but that little would be done, as the telecommunications lobby is so powerful and not going to be stopped by some little local zoning board in the boonies. Moe Mease and Rudy Smith objected to the use of the word "boonies," and Mease questioned why the citizens of Carthage should have to put up with all these flatlanders coming here and knocking off the kids with gamma rays from their (expletive) tower so they can talk to one another from their Volvos.

Zack Glassman, whose grandfather fell in his wheelchair down the stairs and broke his neck in November, walked to the microphone and said he wasn't going to let the federal government stand in the way of doing what was right. He knocked over the microphone and left the Carthage cafeteria with a fist clenched in the air. Others of the young people left the room cursing the federal government, though Chairman Gomes asked them repeatedly to respect the American town governmental process.

When order was restored, Chairman Gomes asked if there were any questions for expert Barrad. There were none. Chairman

Gomes said he and the Carthage Zoning Board of Adjustment would be interested at this time to hear from any other witnesses WIKD would like to put forward. Attorney Messinger asked to replace attorney Baines as spokesperson for WIKD and Nynex. The chairman gave his assent, but attorney Messinger refused to be sworn in to tell the truth. After a caucus, the Zoning Board of Adjustment reconvened and agreed to let attorney Messinger speak regardless of his honesty.

Attorney Messinger of WIKD turned away from the Zoning Board members to address his comments to the citizens of the Town of Carthage and stated that he was not going to waste their time with the complicated fine points of his legal argument but that radio station WIKD had been wronged by Zoning Board Administrator Neil Cato and the Town of Carthage. Attorney Messinger said that the crux of his legal argument was that it was the position of WIKD (and Nynex Mobile, a co-user of the tower) that the Carthage Zoning Board is preempted from dealing with radio-frequency interference because under the Communications Act of 1934 Congress gave away all power to regulate radio waves to the FCC. He repeated that the Town of Carthage had absolutely no right to impede the federally mandated and inviolable freedom of radio waves and thus the present proceedings were spurious and a waste of the time of all present, and he therefore thought that the Notice of Violation should be quickly dismissed and, as good and reasonable people, everyone should just go home and watch TV.

Messinger submitted his legal argument to the Zoning Board members and stated that if the Zoning Board of Adjustment decided to stand by the Notice of Violation of Zoning Board Administrator Cato, WIKD would regretfully be forced to sue the Town of Carthage and all the Zoning Board members individually for damages to his client WIKD, as had been done in other towns successfully across the country, as the legal point was ironclad in his opinion. He also stated those present might do well to consider the many positive benefits of the radio tower and how without the radio tower (and other communication towers like it) the Town of Carthage would lose vital links with the information age and face the grave risk in this day and age of being without information.

Board member Brewster Hutchins asked if attorney Messinger was saying that the board members could lose their dairy farms or homes that had been in their families for generations if the suit for damages was lost, and attorney Messinger said that this was sadly indeed one possible negative outcome. Brewster Hutchins asked if attorney Messinger of WIKD spent a lot of time talking on his cell phone. Attorney Messinger asked what was the point of the question, and Hutchins said he was thinking out loud about what he had heard in the earlier testimony about the relation between radio waves and brain damage.

There was an interruption from the playground of the Carthage Central School, and Bob Hammond came in and said that Zack Blessman and some other youths were firing at the WIKD radio tower in the dark with their hunting rifles but that they were pretty bad shots in general and that it would take a couple of sticks of dynamite at the base of one of the trusses to do the job right, if you asked him. Rudy Smith stated that for the record he had some dynamite in his truck outside.

Chairman Gomes regained control of the meeting, and Maryann Gingus stated she had just received a phone call from her little angel Stacey, direct from her hospital bed in Boston Children's Hospital, and that Stacey wanted to say a few words to all her friends in Carthage. The request was granted after numerous negative comments from the lawyers for WIKD, as the call was received on a cellular phone and attorney Mes-singer wanted pointed out for the record the crucial emergency call was being transmitted through the nearby WIKD tower and that without the benefit of the radio tower the citizens of Carthage would not be able to receive this crucial call from this tragically sick child.

After discussion with expert Barrad it was determined the best way to proceed was to place the microphone next to the mouth end of the cellular phone held by Maryann Gingus. The voice of little Stacey Gingus was heard over some static, and at the sound of her brave voice there was much applause and many tears from the citizens of Carthage. Stacey asked if her hamster Sweet Pea had her babies yet, and Maryann Gingus replied not yet. Stacey also requested a Carthage Little League baseball cap and then said she had something important to say to everyone. There was absolute silence in the Carthage Central School cafeteria, and at this point "gonna make you sweat, gonna make you groove" was transmitted loudly through the microphone. The phrase was identified by Chairman Gomes as lyrics from the song "Black Dog" by Led Zeppelin. Maryann Gingus tried repeatedly to regain communication with her little angel Stacey and after attempting to hit attorney Messinger over the head numerous times with the cellular phone was re-strained and led in a hysterical state from the cafeteria by Chairman Gomes, Zoning Board Administrator Neil Cato, and Dr. Hadley of the Carthage Health Center.

Attorney Baines took the microphone from the floor and stated that under the circumstances WIKD might now be will-ing to consider—while still not acknowledging actual inter-ference from the WIKD tower—replacing up to one small appliance in each household as a gesture of goodwill.

The Spoon Children

LIKE A LOT OF THIS takes place before me and Nosebone got out there to the Anarchist Convention in Portland in the summer of 1996. Maybe you read about the convention in the newspapers, because of the martial law. For me all this time before the convention is kind of like a foggy blur, because before I met Blue out there on the West Coast, I was like tripping six days a week.

Before we left Providence for the West Coast I had some serious dreads, and I had just grown this wispy gold thing on my chin, and I used to curl it in my fingers a lot when I was tripping. I don't know, it just felt good in between my thumb and fingers. Maybe because I was like just sixteen and it was the first hair on my face so it was kind of cool and when you're tripping you can get all meditative like *these are the first hairs on my face*—even if it's not the sort of thing I would've said to Bugeye or Nosebone or any of the other dudes I was skateboarding with in Providence in those days. If Blue was around in those days, I might of said it to her, but she was still in my future.

So anyway, this is the way it all went down. At the time I was living in a big closet in the apartment of this guy Wayne, who was one of the dealers I used to work for, and when I wasn't tripping I'd run errands like get pizza. I was way into acid right then, sometimes I'd spend all day alone in the closet. I remember sweating a lot in there, because the apartment was pretty hot. And then one day I like stumbled out of the closet thinking like: *Water! Water!* And this Irish dude Ian is suddenly there, and he gets me a glass of water and asks me why I'm sweating in the closet. Common-sense question, but it got me thinking. Maybe it was his accent that made me hear him. Ian told me how he had met this American girl in Amsterdam, and how he got all the last of his money and came over to surprise her. She was like, *sorry you came, dude,* and he was pretty down about it. He wouldn't stop talking about the girl that dumped him, and I like didn't want to go back in the closet and sweat, so I sat on the sofa and listened to him a lot. Man, he could talk. I told him I personally thought sex was way overrated, it was like no big deal and kind of boring. That was my opinion, although he tried to convince me otherwise. Ian talked so much about this girl I started to miss her myself eventually, which was pretty trippy.

One day while Ian and I are talking, Wayne the dealer comes storming in and he's all pissed off because the Providence cops have totally cracked down on his business. Wayne is in his twenties, and a big dude, and you pretty much didn't

want to be around when he was pissed off. But this day he
chilled pretty quick, because he started telling me and Ian
about how he was heading to the Anarchist Convention in
Portland, and saying we should join him. Ian said he wanted to
go as far as Minneapolis, and said he'd pay for the gas that far.
Wayne said he'd bring some herb so he could contribute to the
cash on hand by selling on the road. I went out on the street
and found Nosebone and Bugeye, and we all got stoked about
going to the Anarchist Convention, even though we didn't
know anything about it. But we were like, *anarchist, man, cool.*

We were all in this stolen Toyota, me and Nosebone and Bugeye and Wayne and the Irish dude Ian. And we were finally
out of Providence, and then the car died. We had just got into
that little tip of Pennsylvania, and the car was like *cathunk,
cathunk, cathunk.* We rolled into the parking lot of like a Kmart
with this dying car and like all my bliss went out the window.
But Bugeye, he used to hang out with Harley people. He opens
the hood and there I am looking at the car engine like *this is a
totally weird thing, an engine.* I was tripping a little. But Bugeye, he right away yanks out the air filter and holds it up in the
air and says *we've got to change this,* so we are all totally stoked
Bugeye has this talent. I mean, he goes in Kmart and gets an air
filter and like ten minutes later we're off again, and I'm like
looking at Bugeye with like this new respect. Which is weird,
because back in Providence I was like generally pretty down on
motorheads.

So we're back on the road, and this is it, the big road trip.
And I'm feeling so pumped up about us heading to the Anarchist Convention and I need some way to express this good
feeling. So I paint my nails black and put on black mascara and
in a gas station I dye my hair black and I put on this long silk

shirt I have that is like a dress. I'm looking like a total freaker, and I'm out of the bathroom maybe two minutes when the cops squeal up and circle me with a couple of cars and their flashing lights on and they're like grilling me. And there are these movie cameras and lights behind them and I'm like *what the fuck?* And the cops want me to sign a waiver, because this is maybe an episode of like the TV show *Cops*. And the cops don't find anything to bust me for, so the camera dudes are pretty glum and they like stick the camera in my face and ask if I'm like into devil worship or anything like that and I'm like *fuck off, dudes.*

Because it was a stolen car, the others vacated when the cops first circled me. When they came back for me, I got in the car and we hit the road again and we all smoked some herb. We all agreed we're like into seeking peace, but what to do when America is so fucked that there are these dudes out there hoping you're into devil worship? I mean what are you supposed to do, *grow up and join these people?* This causes a momentary downer on our trip, but we take some acid, and then are stoked again all the way to Minneapolis. We get to Minneapolis and go to the house of Ian's friend's father, and it turns out the dude is an FBI agent, only he's not home right then and his wife offers us milk and cookies and insists we all come in, but first we all go out in the backyard and there is this little stream and we stand there in the rain and get stoned and consider our options.

When we go back to the house there is this dude, this totally square Ronald Reagan FBI dude, and we know he can smell the herb all over us, and he's like giving us punks the fake smile and the pleased to meet you. But we're in the house, and he doesn't bust us right away, so we think *what the hell?* We don't tell him we're heading to the Anarchist Convention, and he says we can sleep in the basement. The basement is all mirrored and I am freaked down there like *what have we done now?* Wayne and Nosebone open a bottle of this guy's Wild Turkey they find behind the bar. It's like a hurricane outside, so we're not moving from the basement, and after a while most everyone chills from the Wild Turkey.

I don't like to drink as I like the innocent herb more, so I don't drink much of the Wild Turkey. And I keep looking at these mirrors on the walls while everyone sleeps, and I keep thinking they're one-way mirrors, and it is freaking me out. So in the middle of the night I take my clothes and Wayne's stash of herb and go sleep in the car. And in the middle of the night Mr. FBI comes down and goes through their stuff. They all woke up, but none of them moved. And like the next morning Wayne is seriously pissed at me for like a violation of his privacy in taking the herb, and philosophically he's right and all, but he could of thanked me for saving him from Mr. FBI. What was really surprising about the whole situation was that Nosebone agreed with Wayne, that I had like no right to go through the guy's stuff, that I like violated his space.

That morning Ian the Irish dude hooks up with some of his people, and we say goodbye to him at the bridge to Saint Paul. I tell him I hope he finds another cool girl, but it was the wrong thing to say, as believe it or not he was still seriously down about getting dumped, which surprised me. While we are all standing there at the bridge to Saint Paul, Wayne sees this cave down below in the bank of the Mississippi River. It's like this natural cave, and we crawl down the bank of the Mississippi to take a look, and it is like definitely way cool. Wayne goes into town to get some food and he comes back and we chow and get stoned and watch the Mississippi from the cave and it goes back to raining pretty hard and Nosebone talked a lot about all the outrageous shit that is surely in our future at the Anarchist Convention.

Late that night there are these loons going by in the moonlight, just riding the raging Mississippi, and I think, *that's me and my life, I'm one of those loons.* It sounds corny and all, but at the time Bugeye and I were into it and we made loon calls until we passed out.

When I woke up my feet were wet and Wayne is like building a wall of dirt to keep the Mississippi River out of the cave. I said, like, *dude, we got to get out of here.* And Wayne argues with me, and we waste a lot of time arguing, and then there is like this flash flood thing happening, and we are like up to our knees and scrambling up the mud bank of the Mississippi. And I get up on the bank with Nosebone and Bugeye and Wayne and the cave is like underwater and the rain is like serious. We all get in the car, and we are all like shaking and freaking out and smoking herb fast and furious to take the edge off the death vibe but it isn't working. Wayne is totally freaking out, and he opens the window and starts randomly throwing shit out the window. He mostly throws his own stuff, but then he throws some of ours and that isn't cool. There is some real shit then between us, and Wayne gets out of the car and says he's going to like walk to Oregon. We're like, *no man, get back in the car.* But Wayne is serious, and walks off into the rain and disappears, and I like sit there afterward looking at the rain pounding on the windshield and pretty much decide the next time I like sleep in a riverbank cave and there is a flash flood, I am like definitely not going to stand around and argue with any *Wayne.*

So then we hit the road again and make our way out of Minneapolis and we are all quiet and thinking our own thoughts about the river and almost getting killed and Wayne going off and taking his herb with him. And me and Nosebone and Bug-eye are pretty quiet and then we see that our stash of acid is gone too, it must have gone out the window when Wayne was freaking out or got lost in the general confusion of our exodus. So this is a real downer, as there are a lot of miles ahead to do straight before we get to the Anarchist Convention. So we are doubly down and generally stolid and it is raining and nobody is talking for many hours and miles. And then in the middle of the night we go into this truckers' stop and we see this graffiti in the bathroom that says both Kings, Rodney and Martin, got what they deserved. We come out of the bathroom and I spit the biggest goober Bugeye said he had ever seen on the counter and we are like totally pissed off. This is like Nebraska, and then all of a sudden we look around at all the truckers and it like clicks and we're like *oh shit*. The truckers in their cowboy hats all just stare at us though, and we back out of there and get back on the road and it was cool again in the car, we had the vibe back.

The car we were driving was pretty silly, there were these huge rusted holes in the floor and it was like still raining heavily and so we're like going through the flood and the rain is like spraying up at us, and it was like we were paddling along the road. There was this extraordinary thing soon after we left the truckers' place. The land was all flat as far as you could see and then there were like hundreds of lightning strikes all tearing up the sky all around us but *from the ground up*. For a minute I thought we were tripping. I mean the lightning was starting from the earth and going to the sky. We were the only people out there, so we stopped the car in the middle of the road, and it was like, *this is for us*. There was so much lightning it was creepy but still cool, and Nosebone floored it and we're flying through all this upside-down lightning and it was like nothing could get us or hurt us and that went on for hours and hours, it seemed like.

Then we seemed to wake up and we were in the Rockies. Man, those are some serious mountains. Like I'm beginning to get a sense of how big this country is, you know. We stop at this rest stop up at the top of the pass in the Rockies and there are these old-timers working at the rest stop, men from the local auxiliary something and they give you free coffee and doughnuts to keep you stoked going down the mountains, and they told us all these crazy stories about how this town used to be a lumber town but now all the timber was gone and shit. And the old-timers and us punks agree America is fucked about how she has treated Mother Nature.

Then we are on the road and we just feel like driving, and we're these three kids and I think we must be crazy but then we hit the Pacific and I know we're not crazy and the sun comes out and the fog clears and there is the whole Pacific Ocean. We're way into the ocean and driving along next to the ocean feeling her beautiful vibe, but then there is this helicopter overhead following us along and it ruined the vibe, then we decide to go with it and watch the helicopter with our heads hanging out the window, but their helicopter vibe is so negative we duck off the road and find this winery way back in the woods with these Alaskans running it and they are cool and give us wine even though it concerned them that we're like only sixteen. They had this white husky and Bugeye played with it and we stomped the grapes, and we're totally stoked and pretty drunk and Bugeye wants a vineyard because it's like ancient and with the earth and then Bugeye decides to stay there at the vineyard because that's where he wants to be to work the earth in like this ancient way.

We're like down to just me and Nosebone in the car. And we're sort of totally mellow as we drive up the coast to the Anarchist Convention and after a couple of hours we're thinking about all the old skateboarder dudes back in Providence and big Wayne and even Bugeye like it was a hundred years ago we last saw them all.

And then soon enough we drive right into the main square in downtown Portland. We see a dude or two playing Hackey-Sack, and then just as we park we see this Dumpster catch fire. All these punks come running out of nowhere and start jumping around the flames and there is like this white BMW next to the Dumpster and they are like jumping around and praying the BMW catches fire. And Nosebone and me see these punks jumping around the flames and think *cool, this is like the sign we were looking for, this is the place we were coming to.*

Nobody is really clear on when the Anarchist Convention is going to start, and the definite vibe is it's not cool to ask, as anarchists are pretty much against setting a serious date and time. So when me and Nosebone are not spare-changing we take to wandering around sort of like tourists, and we find this massive old castle thing in the hills up above Portland. This big old stone castle that for some reason they took a wrecking ball to but there is still enough of the walls left so you can see how cool it was once. We decided to move to this like castle up in the hills. We drove around and found all this wood in the Dumpsters at like these huge new mansions under construction outside Portland, and took the wood up to the castle and built a couple of cool shelters.

More and more punks are coming into Portland for the Anarchist Convention, and some of them hear about the castle and they start to come up and build their own shelters. There was this one old guy we called G.I. Joe who was AWOL from the U.S. Army and he was like the mayor of our growing freak city. He stayed up there all the time and watched our stuff when we were down busking for change. A big crew of trainhoppers showed up with spray paint in their hair as it keeps out the lice, they had flashlights and all the gear for trainhopping, and they were all pretty cool. Some of the old guys on the scene start to tell stories about their life on the road around the fire we've got going at night and it's like we're part of this big tribe for a while and these are our old storytellers and it was cool and kind of beautiful if you know what I mean but there was this one guy Frank, he was like fifty years old and a roadie and a juicer and at first he was cool and he told some good stories like the rest of the old guys, but then he got juiced and I ended up like holding his elbow and keeping him from wandering off the cliff all night.

The scene finally started up for the Anarchist Convention. Turns out the anarchist thing goes way back in Portland, it is like where the first convention for communal living was held like fifty years ago. The scene in 1996 was at this café called the Atomic. A grocery store kicked down some food and there was like the first party of the convention at the Atomic, and the truth is mostly we just stood around, all us punks from around the country, waiting for something to happen. There were chips, wine, and everyone was like *where you from, dude?* and then someone would try to get something organized but someone else would call them a fascist and everyone would go back to partying and then someone else would try to get something together like a talk on how to tip over cars, or how to keep a boxcar open, or how to get into Canada on this secret trail, or how to find a good squat and keep the cops off your back, or generally how to live a life separate from the suburban and corporate American power trip, but as soon as someone got a talk going someone would say *bollocks to this, we're anarchists, let's just party.*

There were some bands planned that night at the Atomic and everyone was getting pumped and saying how *we're going to rock the house now* and *burn the place down* because *we're anarchists* but in the end it was just an OK party and everyone was pretty much like looking for something to happen. I was actually getting pretty bored and then there was this like seventy-year-old, wrinkled-up guy who looked like a troll in my face telling me we should do something, so we go in the back and make a huge pot of noodles and he threw all this random stuff in the pot that looked to me kind of rotten and we went back out and fed everyone and they were all reaching in and eating with their hands, but it was cool anyway that the old troll guy had the idea that we feed everyone, because it was clear all the anarchists in general were pretty hungry, and nobody else was going to do anything about it.

If you tried to talk to the anarchists it turned out no one there was actually very interesting, and then I see this bald-headed girl sitting in the back reading the dictionary and I'm thinking she's kind of odd to be reading the dictionary, but I'm also getting this growing vibe as the days pass that maybe I'm kind of crazy myself, and then I saw her looking back at me and she looked kind of cool so I went over and she wanted to cut my dreads to get the lice out. I didn't know I had lice but my head was getting pretty itchy, but still I wasn't ready to give up my dreads quite yet. She wants to play with my hair and I'm like, *whatever,* and then she takes a strand of hair and like ties it onto a ring off her finger and leans back and dangles it over her heart, and because it swings clockwise without her doing anything she says I have a positive vibe for her.

The punk band tries to start up right then but this woman with shaved eyebrows and blue hair gets the mike and she wants to talk about our legal rights as squatters and all sorts of other official anarchist stuff and one punk in the crowd calls her a Nazi bitch and how we're anarchists and how her organizing us is making us militaristic and she drops the mike and walks over and brains him with this bottle and he's gushing blood. Nosebone runs over and is like talking about her freedom to do that to him and then I see the girl with the dictionary is like helping the bleeding guy on the floor and then this tall bald woman in skintight black leather with a staff in her hand and these big blue eyes like pools steps in front of me and she says she came all the way from Finland. The truth is she was kind of a spooky old lady, like a witch or something, and she tells me with her blue eyes boring into me some trippy shit like *you must slay the dragon.* Right then someone says there are two squad cars outside and everyone was trying to hide although it was just a big room and there was no place to hide. People with warrants for their arrest are crawling out the bathroom windows, and then all these guys in the center of the room take out yo-yos. They are these heavy-duty stone yo-yos and these guys are trainhoppers and they use them to fight the bulls on trains. Then someone says the cops are gone and I go over and ask the girl with the dictionary her name. She tells me she has no name, and then says she wants to go to the castle with me. We get in the car and there is only jazz on the radio and I listen to it for a minute and say *I kind of like it* and she says *that's cool,* so we listen to the jazz and drive up to the path to the castle.

The old guys up at the castle tried to get the storytelling thing going again that night, but the scene up there was now overrun with all these straight kids from the suburbs, they were all there hungering for the anarchist vibe. For a while G.I. Joe was showing me how to blow fire with a mouthful of gasoline. He was sending these flames from his mouth like ten feet in the air. At one point I go off to take a piss and while I'm taking a piss the word comes that the scene is about to be raided by the Portland cops and G.I. Joe is yelling for everyone to run for the hills but I run back into the castle area anyway against the general flow of humanity and try and find the girl with no name. G.I. Joe grabs me and says she's already run, so then I get out of there just before the cops overrun the place. G.I. Joe let himself get caught by the Portland cops and put up a big struggle so the rest of us could get away, and they beat him pretty solidly with their nightsticks.

I am hiding up there in the hillside pressed down in the dirt gully listening to the cops beating on G.I. Joe and generally trashing the scene and right in front of my nose which is pressed in the dirt is this silver bracelet and I put it on and think this silver bracelet will protect me. The cops finally leave but the place is totally trashed, all the shelters are knocked down. I never find the girl with no name again that night, although it seems like I drove all over town looking for her and Nosebone.

The next day there are ten bands set to play at the Atomic Café. It's like the high point of the Anarchist Convention. The first band is like setting up their huge speakers when suddenly there are a hundred cops outside. The cops are all in full combat gear, with the flak jackets and shields and helmets and nightsticks. Inside the Atomic Café we are all silent and looking at each other, and then for no reason the cops tear-gas the place. There are a lot of people inside who know what to do about tear gas from their anarchist training, and everyone works together and we have a line from the bathroom wetting down T-shirts so we can put them over our nose and mouth, but it doesn't really work that well, and they shoot in another canister of tear gas, and we all have to stumble outside coughing.

There are like more than a hundred of us punks, and more than a hundred cops. We are standing there in front of the Atomic Café, and nothing is happening except for a lot of coughing from the tear gas, and then a couple of our people raise a banner that says NO WAR BUT THE PEOPLE'S WAR and that sort of gets things going, and we all link arms in four rows and we all start to chant *one love*. That was totally cool, standing there with the other freaks all chanting *one love* at the cops, but then Nosebone and some of the other punks started breaking off chunks of concrete from the sidewalk and passing them out. The owner of the Atomic Café is like freaking out, I guess thinking his place was about to be trashed, and then I saw the girl with no name climbing up a tree off to one side of the scene. She must not have been there earlier, but now she was climbing up this skinny tree. She saw me and gave me the *Power to the people* sign, and I gave it back.

It was then that the local TV news cameras showed up and the weird theater part of that afternoon started up. The older people among us started singing all these anarchist songs from the 1960s, and the rest of us sang along when we caught on, or when the lyrics were obvious. The girl with no name seemed to know all the songs, you could hear her little voice up in the tree. She sang up there like a bluebird. When most people dropped out of a song, she would still be singing up there in the tree. The cops started to take notice of her then, they started pointing their nightsticks at her. She came down from the tree and walked over and led all of us in singing the punk version of the national anthem, with lyrics like *land of the slaves, home of the hypocrites*. The cops started to do some dumb and childish shit as she sang, like stroking their nightsticks in a sexual manner.

The scene is pretty chilled out now, except the cops are still standing there in full combat gear. There was a big crowd of civilians now behind the cops, and they start yelling at the cops that we didn't do anything wrong and that we're not real anarchists at all but just fucked-up kids so to leave us alone. Then someone started to yell, *let's show the people of Portland what we're all about,* and then it happened, everyone started to run for this road. We're like stampeding cattle, and the cops only grab a few of us. I saw one punk down on the ground getting clubbed. I remember I saw the girl with no name ahead of me running down the road. We're all just running down the street in this crazy mob, and I see Nosebone run up the front of a Mercedes, and he *whonked* on the front windshield with his boot, and ran over and *whonked* on the back windshield and broke that too, and there were these people inside the Mercedes screaming. Other punks started throwing bricks and rocks through the windows of these four-star restaurants where people were eating by like romantic candlelight.

I must of run a couple of miles. Then I hid for a couple of hours in a drainage pipe. Then I started to think about the girl with no name, and I kept thinking about her, and then my feet did this crazy thing, they started to walk back toward downtown Portland. It turns out Portland is like under martial law at this point, but I didn't know that yet, so I walked into the street where the whole scene went down at the Atomic Café, and right away these two cops on horses come galloping up, and one grabs me by the arm, and then the other gets my other arm, and they drag me into a side street. I am like screaming at the top of my lungs and then something more important came over their police radio and one of them whacked me on the head with his nightstick and they galloped off.

So I was like sitting in this alley holding my head. And it was dark and I just sat there thinking about the girl with no name. It was like when the cop hit me with the nightstick he knocked everything else right out. It was like I couldn't even remember my childhood life, or my life with the skateboarders in Providence, or the trip across America, or even the castle. I remember I started to laugh right there in the alley while holding my head, because I was now sort of like that Irish dude Ian who came here from Amsterdam because of a girl and couldn't stop thinking about her no matter that she dumped him. So then I hear someone coming down the street, and it is that weird old woman in black leather with the staff and the blue eyes who was sort of like a witch. She like reminds me she told me to *slay the dragon* back at the Atomic that night it was almost raided, but I'm not really in the mood for any of that weird stuff at this point. Before she goes I ask her if she knew what happened to the girl up in the tree, and she says *you mean the princess?* and I think she's like living in this alternative reality, but then she snaps out of it and says she saw her arrested and taken away by the police.

For a couple of hours I just sat there in the alley, then I got up and went in search of some scissors or a knife. I am clued in to the fact now that it is martial law in Portland, so I have to move with care, but I make my way successfully back up to the castle. Only Frank the old juicer is there, but he has a pair of scissors in his pack, and I tell him to cut off all my dreads. He asks me if I want to be a skinhead, and I say, no, I want just a regular suburban haircut. I have to tell him everything before he will agree to do this, and then I see all my dreads fall off me. He once cut hair, so he gives me a pretty decent haircut. Then I go around and look for some half-decent clothes. The castle is a mess from when the cops trashed it, but sure enough I find one half-decent pair of pants, and a decent shirt. Then Frank looks at me and starts to stroke his chin, and I remember my goatee, and with a couple of snips he takes it right off.

So as now I look pretty straight I am free to walk right through downtown Portland without any hassle. And I go to the police station and they tell me they have a girl who won't give her name, and I tell them *that's my sister.* I sit there and wait to see what happens, and the cops are eventually pretty nice to me, because without the dreads and the goatee I look like just another boring suburban kid. And it was while I was sitting there staring at the wall of the police station that I get this weird new vibe, so then I ask the cops and they tell me her bail is set at like a hundred dollars. I like hit the streets. Because of the martial law, there are like no other punks spare-changing, so I have like the whole marketplace to myself. Also I looked like a totally straight suburban kid now, so I was able to go with the *quarter for a phone call?* and the people of Portland were totally cool. The suburban kid thing worked so well that I found these schoolbooks, put them under my arm, and hit the people up for bus fare. It took like two days of total commitment, but I like raised the bail. And it was after spare-changing all day, while spending nights at the police station drinking their coffee, that I started to write some poems for the girl with no name and most of them were pretty stupid, but some were pretty cool.

So I paid the bail, and I was heavily into writing this one poem late one night, when I see the girl with no name walk out from behind the police desk. She's like standing there looking at me like I'm totally crazy, and then she runs over and starts feeling my dread-less head. She finds out that I raised her bail, and that I cut my dreads for her, and I show her the poems I wrote for her, and she's like *I've never had a friend like you.* I remember the silver bracelet on my wrist, and I give it to her and tell her that as long as she wears it, I will always keep her safe. I don't know what got me talking like that, it just happened. It was like I was suddenly totally transformed into Ian the Irish dude, if that makes any sense.

And then we went up to the castle, and Frank the juicer was gone along with all the other anarchists, and we stayed up there all night and looked down at the lights of Portland. I told her at one point about the upside-down lightning we saw in Nebraska, and how Nosebone floored it and how we were like flying through all this upside-down lightning and it was like nothing could ever get us or hurt us. I told her I had the same vibe sitting next to her there at the castle. We talked a lot about the various strange forces at work in the world, and then at dawn she turns to me and tells me to name her, and I picture her up in the tree singing anarchist songs like a bluebird and so I shorten that general idea and name her *Blue.* And then as the morning sun is like in our eyes blinding us we start talking about sex and I tell her about my opinion that sex is boring and just a slam and she didn't laugh at me but changed my mind on that score like totally that morning up at the castle, and that new like energy that came with the sex with Blue led directly to some other things.

Like that morning we decided to head for Mexico. But first at Blue's suggestion I left the stolen Toyota outside the Portland police station with a note on the windshield that said, *very sorry I stole this car.* We didn't want that negative karma following us to Mexico.

It turns out that Blue has a little operating cash as well as a guitar, and on the bus I like strummed the guitar and tried to turn some of the poems I wrote about her in the police station into songs. I knew like some chords, and I made up these songs. So like a week later we are in this restaurant in Tijuana, and this old Mexican lady saw the guitar in my hand and asked me to play a song. There were these punks with us that we met in Tijuana, and they heard me start to play and strum this song all about Blue, and being into head-banging music they're all like *what the fuck with the acoustic shit, man.* But the old Mexican lady was into the song, and she bought me and Blue our dinner that night, and that was definitely cool, and got me to thinking pretty hard.

What happened next was I bought this harmonica, and I sort of learned how to play it. And then one day instead of busking for change with the other punks, I like went to another street with Blue, and I played my guitar and my harmonica, and I was like suddenly this carnival, man, this walking carnival. And I like put out this silly hat that I had been wearing on my head, and started making like eighty to a hundred pesos an hour. And Blue learned how to play spoons so we called ourselves the Spoon Children. And when I looked out at the street crowd when I played I was surprised to see all these *touristos* were totally getting their heads around our music.

So things for Blue and I have been generally pretty righteous ever since, but at least twice a day I wonder what happened to Nosebone.

The Hotel on
Monkey Forest Road

WE HAD STUMBLED out of a monsoon into the Rangoon
bar earlier that evening. Most of us were American and British
engineers, consultants to the Aussies, who were opening a
nickel mine on the Tessarim coast; a couple of the French were
with the Libyans, who were mining uranium up in Chauk. The
old Canadian guy was already sitting down at the end of the bar
when we showed up, and at first only let on he was here in
Myanmar building a hotel on Letsok-Aw, an island down the
Mergui Archipelago.

The story he told us that night was about a hotel project he
had worked on a few years back in Ubud, Bali. I had been to
the beach at Kuta in Bali surfing the pipes in my wandering
twenties, and had driven north in a *bemo* for a day at Ubud. It
was north of the airport at Denpasar, in the layered emerald

rice fields beneath the sacred mountains of Batur and Agung. At first all I remembered about Ubud was that Hindu priests had fled there a thousand years ago when the rest of Indonesia was overrun by Islam, and that Ubud was still virginal, in comparison to the southern peninsula of Bali, which in fifteen years had evolved into a Buddhist Fort Lauderdale.

The Canadian, who said his name was Sherm Strickhauser, went to Ubud to build a hotel for the Crown Royal hotel chain out of Singapore. He proudly rattled off some of the places he'd built hotels for Crown Royal over the last thirty years: Belize, Madagascar, Tobago, Thailand, Irian Jaya . . . the list went on. Sherm kept repeating how he and his best friend, Andrew Rouse, had always kept their Crown Royal hotel projects "ahead of schedule and under budget." He pounded the bar a lot with his fist and said the two of them "always ran a tight ship."

Besides being his best friend, Andrew Rouse was also Sherm's boss. For twenty years Andrew and Sherm had been an international Fred Flintstone and Barney Rubble while their wives, Wilma and Betty, had hung out together in Toronto until the boys winged back from pouring concrete over the globe. But just before the Bali project, Andrew Rouse had fallen for a Danish airline stewardess twenty-five years younger. Sherm thought it was just a bloody fling that had ended after their last project, but then Andrew disappeared from Toronto for a week and showed up in Bali with the stewardess, Victoria Ericksen, literally on his back. This woman in the white tank top was riding piggyback on Andrew as they came out of customs in Denpasar, and Andrew grabbed Sherm by the arm and led them toward a *bemo* for the bumpy ride up to Ubud.

Victoria sat in Andrew's lap all the way to Ubud. Sometimes she'd stick her pinkie in his mouth and he'd pretend to bite it. As they bumped over the potholes Victoria showed Sherm she had no fingernails on her pinkies. Victoria also told Sherm about how she and Andrew had just spent an incredible week helicopter skiing in the Canadian Rockies.

When they got to Ubud at sunset, the two jumped out of the *bemo* and ran into the jungle like a couple of kids. Sherm stood on the road above and watched them laughing their way down to the golden river far below. There were monkeys chattering like lunatics in the trees over his head. Andrew and Victoria took off their clothes and lay down in the shallow river. Then Andrew stood up naked as a jaybird in the river and while pointing to his nose yelled up to his old friend Sherm, "Smell the perfume? The air here is perfume!"

At this point in his story, Sherm looked around at all of us engineers in the Rangoon bar and sniffed the air with disgust.

Sherm shook his head and ordered another Malang beer from the toothless bartender. And then at my prompting he went on with his story about his old best friend, Andrew Rouse, the Danish stewardess Victoria Ericksen, and the construction of the Crown Royal hotel in Ubud.

The original plan was to put up the hotel and twenty villas on Monkey Forest Road. Everyone who has been to Ubud has walked down Monkey Forest Road. I was mildly surprised to hear they were building a hotel there—it was some of the only jungle land left around Ubud. Every other inch around Ubud has been elegantly terraced emerald rice paddies for at least the last thousand years. There's another thing I remembered about Bali as Sherm told his story—how every single drop of water from the mountains was channeled down the hillsides from rice paddy to rice paddy. The whole crazily elaborate Balinese culture was organized around worshiping this sacred water from the mountains.

But back to his story: Andrew and Victoria and Sherm and the other members of the Crown Royal construction management team rented a row of rooms at Poppie's Guest House, and they hired hundreds of Balinese and began to order construction supplies from Jakarta and Melbourne. I should say Sherm did the hiring of the Balinese workers and the ordering of building supplies, because according to Sherm, Andrew and Victoria spend their days wandering around the rice paddies of Ubud as if stoned out of their heads. Although Sherm didn't agree and got pissed off when I suggested it, from what I remembered, Ubud *was* one remaining place on the globe where the culture and landscape could still alter your sense of reality—it was a certified Shangri-la.

So anyway, one day the bulldozers arrive up from Denpasar on flatbeds, and the next morning the workers are ready to scrape out the roads and foundation sites on the forty-acre jungle hotel site. Andrew Rouse is nowhere to be found on this day, but it is pretty clear what needs to be done to the site, as by now the jungle is all surveyed and staked out. But then Andrew comes roaring up to the site on this 350cc motorcycle with Victoria. He says he's got a major announcement for the construction team. Andrew looks serious, like he is about to lay on them the ten commandments, and then takes a deep breath and says he's decided, after a great deal of thought, that the construction management team should wear sarongs "to exhibit their cultural sensitivity."

Rather than start bulldozing that day, Andrew walked the nine incredulous Western men back up Monkey Forest Road to Ubud, where he supervised the purchase of sarongs. When all the men were fitted out like parrots, he walked them to a local Balinese house. The lady of the house led them all from room to room while Victoria explained how the house was set up like the human body. At the entrance or "head" was a shrine to the ancestors, and the living areas were on either side like the arms, and the kitchen was farther in, and out back was the asshole—the garbage dump. Andrew took them back around to the front of the house and pointed up toward Mount Agung, and said the ancestors' temple, or head of the house, always pointed toward the sacred mountain, as this direction was *kelod,* or good, and the asshole of the house pointed toward the sea, as this direction was *kaja,* or evil. Rain came from the mountains, rain had given the people rice and life for thousands of years, thus the mountain and its rain were good.

Andrew and Victoria completed this baffling lesson and then hopped on their motorcycle and took off for a pilgrimage to Mount Agung. The next day after breakfast Andrew came in with the architectural plans and dramatically tore them up in front of the Crown Royal men. He then led the men back to the Monkey Forest Road site, and had the men raise their palms and try to "get an intuitive feel" for "the best vibrational zones" for the placement of the villas. He said they were going to start from scratch, build the villas facing in the *kelod* direction. Sherm said the other men didn't mutiny and went along with this crazy shit because he made the mistake of asking them to, as a personal favor to him.

At first, on the next, steamy morning, Andrew seemed his old all-business self when he rushed everyone down Monkey Forest Road for a dawn start. But a couple of the guys came late in Western clothes, and Andrew sent them back for their sarongs. So eventually all the men were standing in sarongs near the river in a heavy mist, listening to the chatter of monkeys when as if on cue thousands of brightly colored birds erupted shrieking from the jungle, and then these young Balinese girls came down a path out of the jungle mist and started passing out colored rice cakes. After them come these old Balinese men playing gamelan tinkle-tinkle music, and then some beautiful half-naked women with four-foot-tall towers of fruit on their heads sashay down, and then two guys carrying roosters in cages of bamboo come running out of the jungle.

Andrew Rouse stepped forward and explained to the men that, according to Balinese custom, before they begin construction of the hotel they have to make a blood sacrifice to the evil spirits. Then this old Balinese guy comes silently out of the woods in a white robe with his hair done up in a little silver knot on top of his head. He's chanting mantras and sprinkling holy water on the men. The roosters are removed from their cages and pushed together, but they refuse to fight. The holy man—called a *pedenda*—he looks on, shaking his head as if this is seriously a bad omen. So the gamelan musicians get a big basket and put the roosters in it. Ten seconds later one of the roosters is dead from a sharpened spur to the heart. The *pedenda* muttered some prayers holding the dead rooster up in his hand, and this Balinese kid named Wayan translated the *pedenda*'s prayers from Bahasa Indonesian for Victoria, who explained to the men, "The holy *pedenda*'s prayers are like a ladder inviting the good spirits to descend, and the music and sacred dances of the women and girls are here to welcome the visiting deities."

This is when Sherm finally spoke up and said to Victoria, "We're the visiting deities here, sister."

Sherm was proud of this one-liner, you could see that. He ordered a shot for all of us in the bar that night in Rangoon and we all drank to the wisdom of this line a few times. That night at Poppie's Guest House the men of the Crown Royal construction team kept repeating his one-liner, describing over and over the look of hatred on the stewardess Victoria's face when Sherm said to her his immortal line, *We're the visiting deities here, sister.*

The next day, when Andrew Rouse again failed to show up to bulldoze the jungle, the men looked to Sherm to take over and give the work order. There were a couple hundred Balinese workers there, too, all looking at Sherm to take over command of the troops. But Sherman couldn't bring himself to give the work order, and took off to find his best friend Andrew Rouse. You could tell one thing as Sherm told us this story in the Rangoon bar—he seriously regretted not giving the order to start construction on that particular day. "If I'd had any brains left in this old head I would have lowered the boom on Andrew right then," said Sherm.

Sherm found Andrew in the house of the village *pedenda* and took Andrew outside and tried to knock some sense into him. He said he didn't come down too hard on his friend because for over twenty years it had always been Andrew who had always cut Sherm slack or covered his ass when he screwed up, and plus, he didn't see the point in alienating his friend totally over what he still read as a midlife crisis. As Sherm tried to bring his friend around to at least talking about hotel construction, Andrew kept glancing up at Mount Agung and finally told Sherm he was waiting for the *pedenda* to pick an auspicious day to begin construction. Andrew kept smiling at Sherm and said how he understood from Victoria that Sherm wasn't totally convinced about his new "low-impact" methods (Sherm called them "no-impact" to big laughs that night in Rangoon), and that although it might seem impossible to believe he and Victoria *had* stepped off the plane in Denpasar and become drugged by Bali and its landscape, and as a result had decided that on *this* construction project they would try to prove that building a hotel does not have to be culturally confrontational or overly destructive.

Sherman had all the engineers pounding the bar when he quietly told how he asked his friend Andrew Rouse at this point, "And it wouldn't be bloody confrontational if a bunch of saronged Balinese showed up at the Queen's Park in Toronto and started bulldozing the place for their resort?"

As we all laughed at this one-liner, Sherman just stared blankly at us. It wasn't funny to him. He leaned forward and said to me while the others around us laughed, "Andrew Rouse was my best friend. All I wanted was for him to get his head out of his ass. So I made the mistake of giving him enough rope to hang himself and kept the Crown Royal management in Singapore in the dark about how this Victoria was messing with his head." Sherm leaned closer and tapping me on the arm said, "But it was *me* who had his head up his ass. *I* let my best friend of twenty years down. "

What Sherm said happened next seems pretty typical, if you have ever worked for an international company in a Third World country. If there is one thing Bali has it is fruit. I remember there were guavas, mangoes, pineapples, papayas, bananas, but there were also horny green durians and blimpings and a dozen other oddities jumping out of the volcanic soil. As for oranges, Bali already had three different kinds. But according to Sherm, Crown Royal Hotels of Singapore insisted on shipping in two dozen Florida orange trees air freight from Indian River. It was like shipping ice to Eskimos.

So the orange trees show up about a week later, while Andrew Rouse was still waiting patiently for the village *pedenda* to proclaim an auspicious day to begin construction. As Sherm had always been in charge of the landscaping on all their previous hotel projects, on the day the trees show up, Sherm grabs some of the happily snoozing Balinese workers and a backhoe and plants the trees as per the old landscaping plans. The orange trees came with a triple dose of good old American chemical fertilizer, so Sherm doped up the soil around them. For the next week he invented reasons for Crown Royal management in Singapore why construction on the hotel hadn't begun, and then the next week he began to submit false reports about how the roads and foundations were in and construction was coming along slowly but steadily. And every day when he saw Andrew he tried to talk some sense into him, but he still didn't come down too hard, because he still thought the right thing to do was cover his friend's ass, and hope when Andrew was tired of screwing Victoria he'd get his head screwed on straight.

Sherm usually took to taking a hammock down to the river after faxing his false noon progress report to Singapore. One day he sees Victoria and Andrew running down the riverside. Andrew comes charging up to him holding out an orange the size of a softball, and starts going on to Sherm how the orange trees from Florida didn't have any fruit when they arrived, but now three weeks later they were giving off these massive oranges. Victoria takes the orange from Andrew and waving it in Sherm's face says how this very orange in her very hand is proof of the sacred fertility of the Balinese soil.

Sherm said how he tried to explain to the two of them that the orange trees did have small oranges on them when they arrived from Florida and that he had hopped them up with a fertilizer cocktail powerful enough to propel the trees to the moon, never mind juicing out a couple of oranges. But Andrew and Victoria wouldn't listen to logic, and they walked up the riverbank with the orange held before them as if it was the Hope diamond.

The next day the surprising word came that the *pedenda* had decreed it was a good day to build a hotel. Sherm ran around gathering the remaining Balinese workers, many of whom had headed back to their villages or Denpasar. When Sherm walked down Monkey Forest Road to the construction site, he found Andrew was already directing the bulldozers through the jungle. It was then that Sherm spotted a half dozen Balinesian workers chomping happily on Florida oranges from the trees he planted. Andrew noticed the orange-eaters at the same moment, and jumped off the bulldozer and ran over to the workers with the translator kid, Wayan, and told the workers in no uncertain terms that *no one* was to eat the oranges from the special Florida trees. Most of the workers ran off, but one old Balinese guy planted his feet, adjusted his yellow-and-silver sarong, and spit a rind at Andrew Rouse's feet before turning and walking slowly off.

Andrew and Sherm worked until sunset that first day. And the next day Sherm and Andrew worked hard together again, just like the good old days, and then about noon Sherm heard yelling and ran over to the orange grove. The old Balinese guy who had spit out the rind the day before was standing in front of the trees with a grinning mouth bulging with Florida orange. At his feet were a dozen half-eaten oranges. Suddenly Andrew was truly the old ass-kicking take-no-prisoners Andrew Rouse. Sherm said he almost broke into a jig as Andrew cursed the grinning old *eater-of-magical-oranges*.

But when Andrew went back to the bulldozers, Sherm saw the old Balinese guy reach up and pluck another orange. The old guy grinned at Sherm and then prowled around tearing orange after orange from the trees and tossing them over his shoulders. A couple of hours later, while everyone was taking a water break, the interpreter kid, Wayan, came up screaming. Andrew Rouse followed Wayan at a trot, and behind them ran a couple dozen curious Balinese workers. Sherm figured it was about all the oranges yanked off the orange trees, but when he got there he saw the ground around the trees was squirming with iridescent green-and-yellow snakes.

Sherm said he immediately grabbed a machete from one of the workers and waded in there among the snakes and started hacking off their heads. He said he'd never felt so angry and didn't give a shit if the snakes were poisonous. And then, as snake heads were flying, he felt someone grab his arm on a backswing of the machete, and it was Andrew, pulling him away from the snakes, saying how they'd try to deal with the snakes in a peaceable fashion.

At Poppie's Guest House that night, Andrew and Victoria walked over to Sherm during dinner. The two asked to sit down and Sherm waved to the empty seats. Sherm said he was pretty depressed at this point, after thinking when Andrew ripped into the old orange eater that his best friend was over his midlife crisis. That evening in Ubud, Andrew Rouse took a long time explaining, as the cicadas sent up this roar, how he had talked it over with Victoria and the village *pedenda,* and they had determined that the snakes appeared in the orange grove because he, Andrew Rouse, had restricted access to the oranges. Andrew said he had learned from the *pedenda* that he had acted in an evil manner by yelling at the old Balinese man and the other local workers for eating the oranges, and that the snakes were a manifestation of his evil action. He went on and on about how it was very important Sherm understand that there was a delicate balance of good and evil on Bali, but Sherm tuned him out after a while and listened to the roar of the cicadas.

The village *pedenda* also convinced Andrew Rouse that the best course of action, given the snakes in the orange grove, was to hold off on construction again until the *pedenda* gave the word that the various deities had been properly propitiated and the balance of good and evil was—well, balanced. Given the general aura of something going awry, the cheery Balinese workers were growing noticeably dour, and then the guards posted at night to protect the machinery at the Monkey Forest Road site started reporting seeing *leyaks*—evil spirits—in the trees of the surrounding jungle. Apparently the Balinese Hindu workers took *leyaks* very seriously, because most of the remaining workers packed up and left Ubud.

In a strange way, Sherm said, he was pleased by the appearance of the *leyaks*, because then at least he could be straight with the Crown Royal management in Singapore and report *something* truthful about what was slowing down the Ubud project—not that he, Sherman Strickhauser, believed in *leyaks* for a second, but it was the *truth* that the superstitious Balinese workers were *leaving* Ubud. Sherm also was pleased to be able to quickly solve the problem of the *leyaks*, as he immediately started importing Muslim workers from Lombok and Java and other Indonesian islands. The Muslims didn't buy easily into *leyak* superstitions.

One afternoon, after signing up another *bemo* load of deadly serious Muslims, Sherm headed to the river to take a bath. When he got down there he found a couple of dozen Westerners busily setting up a fashion shoot for CNN. Out of the crowd milling around the silver light reflectors came Victoria. She came right up to Sherm and said, "You're trying to hurt Andrew, aren't you?"

Sherm shook his head. He was flabbergasted. All he wanted was for his friend Andrew to pull his shit together and not throw away his job. He said he just stood there shaking his head.

"You think it's me," said Victoria.

Sherm was still so pissed off at this woman that he just shook his head again.

"Yes, you do," said Victoria.

Sherm finally found his tongue and said, "I've known the guy since before you were born."

Victoria said, "Yes, well, you don't know your friend that well. Andrew is making up his own mind here."

"Bullshit," said Sherm.

"Every day Andrew is more alive," said Victoria. "I watch him coming alive faster and faster."

Victoria took a step closer to Sherm, put her hand on his shoulder, and added, "Everyone feels the negative energy you carry, Sherman. Your vibrations precede you like a storm. You need to open up a little, expand your sensitivities."

Victoria walked away from Sherm, and then he took note of the gold Rolex on her wrist. He called after her, "Nice watch." Victoria turned on the path, and Sherm said his next famous one-liner, "I'll tell you one thing I know for sure—'sensitivities' didn't buy that Rolex on your wrist, princess."

Sensitivities didn't buy that Rolex struck a chord with the crowd of engineers in the Rangoon bar that evening. When things quieted down, Sherm went on with his story. He told how right after his zinger line, he sees all these models coming down the side of the river, the models being led down the river-bank by none other than the old orange-eating Balinese coot. Sherm decided to stand around and watch the fashion shoot, but as soon as the models start splashing around like children in the river, the skies blacken up and there is a dramatic down-pour. Sherm vaguely saw the director of the shoot run through the sheets of rain over to the old orange-eating Balinese guy and enter into a serious powwow. There was a model next to him, and Sherm asked her what the director was asking the old Bali-nese guy about, but she just shook her head. Then the old Bali-nese guy starts spinning around on the shore of the river like a dervish. For an old guy he was really kicking up his heels. Everyone from the CNN shoot watched the old guy spinning with a serious-as-shit look on their faces. Sherm asked a Ger-man model, and she said the old orange eater was a locally fa-mous witch doctor called a *balian,* and that the director of the fashion shoot had hired the old guy to stop the rain.

The old Balinese guy danced in the rain. The fashion-shoot crowd slowly drifted away from the old guy dancing on the riverbank, and scrambled up the muddy hillside on their hands and knees in twos and threes. Sherm and the German model were the last ones to leave, and when Sherm looked down from the top of the riverbank through the shifting sheets of rain, the old guy was still dancing alone down there.

As Sherm walked up Monkey Forest Road he bumped into Andrew Rouse and was suddenly so pissed that he was barely able to speak, but he managed to push out another one-liner: "Witch doctor, down by the river, dancing to stop the rain—you probably want to check it out."

Sherm banged his fist over the laughter of the engineers in the Rangoon bar. "And right when my best friend, Andrew

Rouse, goes down to the river and sees the witch doctor dancing, what the hell happens?"

"The bloody rain stopped!" yelled one of the engineers.

All the engineers in the Rangoon bar sympathized with this bad luck. It was obvious to all that for a guy with his head up his ass as far as Andrew Rouse, this sort of bullshit coincidence of the rain stopping was bound to lead to more trouble.

The engineers groaned when all the candles suddenly blew out in the Rangoon bar. The bartender hobbled over and angrily slapped the wooden shutters shut on the windows. As the bartender looked for a match back in the rear, Sherm told us in the dark how the next day when he showed up at the Monkey Forest Road construction site with a cup of java in hand, he saw his best friend standing in the orange grove with the same old rain-dancing, orange-eating Balinese *balian*.

When Sherm walked over to the *balian* and Andrew Rouse that morning, he noticed the orange grove was still full of the squirming yellow-and-green snakes. He didn't have to tell us engineers what was going on: Andrew Rouse had hired the old *balian* to get rid of the snakes. Sherm said he was finally going to take off the gloves, try one last time to shake up his old friend. Sherm said he had gotten a fax from Crown Royal management that morning telling him he had better get the project up to speed or they were sending a troubleshooter from Singapore, and he and Andrew would be on the next plane to Toronto.

But just as Sherm walked up to Andrew Rouse that morning, the old Balinese *balian* slipped off his sandals and stepped in among the snakes. Sherm had heard that the snakes were puff adders and deadly poisonous. The *balian* stood there amidst the snakes in his bare feet, and soon workers were running from all directions to see the performance. The *balian* closed his eyes—though Sherm was sure he was looking—and started to walk back and forth among the snakes. Sherm decided the old coot was going to get himself killed and went forward, yelling at the bastard to get the bloody hell out of there, but Andrew ran over and grabbed him by the arm and told him to let the *balian* work. The *balian* bent over and appeared to be talking to the snakes, and then he raised his arms and danced among the snakes. Sherm said the *balian* was doing the same tired dance routine he'd done to stop the rain. Then the *balian* reached down and snatched a snake from the ground and wrapped it around his neck. He now danced facing the crowd, motioning with his hands as if he was asking them to join him in his snake-charming dance.

Sherm said the dance went on way too long, and that he suddenly couldn't stop laughing. He said he laughed because the other snakes were sunbathing and ignoring the dancing old coot, and he was sure at that moment that after twenty years of busting his ass for Crown Royal, he was about to lose his job because of this crazy old snake charmer. The old *balian* heard him laugh, stopped dancing, and opened one eye and surveyed Sherm from among the snakes. The *balian* said something quickly to the kid translator, Wayan, who ran over to Andrew Rouse and whispered in his ear. Then Sherm saw Andrew Rouse open his wallet and start handing over rupiah. Sherm watched as the old *balian* made a small pile of the rupiah on the ground, whipped out a lighter from nowhere, and started burning the cash. He fanned the flames and motioned for more cash from Andrew, who without hesitation ran over among the snakes and kept feeding him the money.

Sherm stopped at this point in his story, and at the same

moment the bartender found a match and lit a candle. Sherm looked around at all us expatriate engineers as if he wanted us to finish this part of the story, and one engineer yelled out, "And a couple of hours later, no bloody snakes!"

Sherm pointed at the engineer who had yelled the right answer, and downed a shot with his free hand. There was some sympathy expressed to Sherm at the bad luck of the snakes vamoosing, strengthening as it clearly would his best friend Andrew Rouse's growing delusions.

Sherm raised his hand, and the engineers grew quiet. The monsoon was rattling the windows as if there were *leyaks* out there in the streets of Rangoon. Sherm had a puffy drinker's face, and the flickering candlelight coming from almost under his chin didn't flatter. He didn't look like the same hearty beef-faced Canadian guy he did with the fluorescent lights on. He almost could have been a *leyak* himself, there in the candlelight at the end of the bar.

And then one of the engineers yelled out, "What about Victoria?"

Sherm nodded and went on with his story and said neither Andrew Rouse nor Victoria showed up at Poppie's Guest House for dinner that evening. After the sun set, the kid translator, Wayan, came to him out of the shadows as he sat drinking scotch on the porch, and said Victoria wanted to see him at the construction site. Sherm walked down Monkey Forest Road with a flashlight. He said there was the smell of burning pig in the air. He heard a *kul-kul* drum beating in a banyan tree from a nearby village. I remembered those drums: Each Balinese village had its own *kul-kul* drum language, although I had heard that fewer and fewer young Balinese could understand their village drum as it spoke to them.

When Sherm got to the construction site he found Victoria

sitting on a bulldozer talking to one of the Muslim guards. The guard faded away as Sherm came up to her. Without saying a word, Victoria handed Sherm a dog-eared pamphlet. He shined the flashlight on the handwritten cover and read in English under the Bahasa Indonesian: *How to Stop the Rain.*

"The *balian's* book," said Victoria in the dark. "Andrew's gone off with him for the night."

"You didn't go?"

"I told you already, Sherman. It isn't me."

"Where's Andrew?"

"The *balian's* going to purify him tonight up at his village. The ritual's supposed to take all night."

Sherm said the way she spoke, it didn't take a rocket scientist to figure out she was no longer too pleased with her middle-aged lover-boy, Andrew Rouse.

Victoria was quiet for a while, sitting there in the bulldozer. Sherm said he could still hear the *kul-kul* drum in the distant banyan tree. Without another word to Victoria, Sherm left the construction site. As he made his way back up to Poppie's Guest House, he came on the kid, Wayan, and asked him if he knew where this *balian* lived. At first Wayan didn't want to talk, but Sherm kept peeling off rupiah in the darkness, and eventually the kid whispered, *"I know where."*

Sherm said he grabbed his bottle of Dewar's off the porch at Poppie's and jumped in a Suzuki jeep with the kid. He spun out of Ubud and bounced along a narrow road up to a village called Penestanan. Wayan then led him among the rice paddies, along a path that was like a maze. A couple of times he stepped off the path and sank up to his knees in the mud.

The old *balian* lived in a shack of sticks and mud. There was the faint glow from a kerosene light inside. When Sherm knocked, the old *balian* came to the door, and started grinning away when he saw Sherm, who figured he was thinking, *Another Western sucker here to pay me to stop the rain.* The *balian* invited Sherm inside, where he tripped over a chicken. There were pigs in the hut too, running around with half a dozen naked kids. Sherm shone his flashlight on the wall, on all these Balinese calendars and astrological charts. Then he saw his friend lying on a cot in the back. Sherm said the old coot had him in some sort of trance where he was just grinning away, staring into space. Andrew slowly rolled his eyes upward as Sherm played the light near his face and repeated over and over how he wanted Sherm to understand how for the first time in his life he felt in harmony with all living things.

Sherm didn't want to listen to this crazy shit, and got Andrew standing with a lot of cursing and dragged him out of the shack. The old *balian* just stood there grinning like an idiot, and the pigs squealed underfoot. Sherm said that as he dragged him down the path Andrew was totally out of his head, and kept trying to explain to Sherm shit like how the *balian* had said things had gone wrong on the project "because we're out of touch with the spirits."

Andrew Rouse was in his own world all the way back to Poppie's Guest House. Sherm said he kept trying to sing some goddamned Balinese song but knew only about three lines. Wayan tried to help him out, until Sherm told Wayan to knock it the hell off. Andrew stopped singing to announce to Sherm, as if it was supposed to be great news, that the *balian* had promised to come to Monkey Forest Road in the morning to seal off the site with energy lines and drive away the negative spirits. When they pulled up to Poppie's Guest House, and Sherm turned off the jeep, Andrew Rouse jumped out and stripped off his clothes and said he was heading down to the river to pray to the goddess Rangda and added over his shoulder, as he took off at a trot down the road, how his one wish now was that Sherm understood what was happening to him.

"Sherm understood!" yelled one of the engineers. "You've fucking gone local!"

"Bloody *loco!*" yelled another engineer, banging his shot glass on the bar for a refill. Soon all the engineers were banging on the bar with their shot glasses. When I shut my eyes it sounded strangely like my memories of a *kul-kul* drum in a banyan tree.

To the engineers that night in Rangoon it was clearly time to ship Andrew Rouse home to Toronto. Heads nodded when Sherm said that the morning after Andrew Rouse went streaking to the river for a quick prayer to the goddess Rangda, Crown Royal Hotels called to fire him and put Sherm in charge of the Monkey Forest Road project.

After he got the word he was in charge, Sherm headed out from Poppie's Guest House to find his friend. He found him down at the Monkey Forest Road site, running like a lunatic after the *balian,* who was charging around the grounds, waving what looked like a tennis racket covered with long colored strings. Sherm figured this must have been the *sealing off of the energy lines and driving away the negative spirits* that Andrew was all excited about the night before. Sherm yelled over to Andrew, who glanced at him but kept charging after the *balian.* At least, Sherm thought, he's got his clothes on now. He couldn't tell his best friend he was fired if the guy didn't have his clothes on. He decided to tell Andrew later, and gathered together a couple dozen workers and a bulldozer and headed up to the north end of the property. There was still a lot of flattening to do up there; it had been called off by Andrew when he realigned the design plans on *kelod* lines. Sherm got to work and tried to put out of his mind what he was going to tell Andrew, but suddenly after pushing down some trees with the bulldozer they found their access to one of the villa sites blocked by a few large boulders. It was going to be a bitch moving them, and Sherm was considering dynamite when the *balian* rushed by waving his tennis racket, followed by Andrew and Victoria.

According to the *balian,* as translated by the kid Wayan, the boulders were an ancient *pura dalem* shrine—one so ancient the primitive carvings were barely visible, although the *balian* ran his fingers over the stone as if reading braille.

Sherm said he didn't know why he didn't tell Andrew he was fired right then. Instead he listened to his friend go on and on about how it wasn't their right to destroy the ancient sacred property of the Balinese. Suddenly Victoria interrupted Andrew to say *she* thought the boulders should go. Sherm said (to big laughs in the Rangoon bar) he figured Victoria was thinking in her pretty head *It's either these rocks, or no more helicopter skiing for me and Andrew in the Canadian Rockies.*

While Andrew Rouse explained his view of things to Victoria, Sherm had a big idea, and sent the kid Wayan off with a mashed handful of rupiah notes and told the kid to find the village *pedenda* and drag him out here into the bush. The *pedenda* came running up the jungle path fifteen minutes later, and Sherm took him aside and laid rupiah on him until the *pedenda* suddenly had an inspiration.

The holy village *pedenda* said in his opinion it would be OK to transfer the spirits in this ancient shrine into a temporary structure until Crown Royal Hotels was able to build a large temple to house the old spirits properly. Sherm winked at us all in the Rangoon bar and asked us if we could guess who was told he'd get the permanent cushy job as *pedenda* in this new temple?

So under the *pedenda*'s excited direction, the workmen built a temporary spirit holder in an hour—it looked, Sherm said, just like an oversized birdcage. With another ten minutes of hocus-pocus the *pedenda* had plucked the ancient spirits out of the stone shrines and popped them into the birdcage. Victoria was so excited—she must have figured there was still a chance Andrew wouldn't lose his job—she asked to carry the birdcage back to the *pedenda*'s house back in the village, where the spirits would reside until the new temple was built. Andrew Rouse sat down on the jungle floor as if exhausted, and watched Victoria walk away with the birdcage down the freshly torn-up road.

Victoria tripped on a root on the way back to the village and crushed the birdcage under her. The *balian* had followed right behind her. Sherm said the old witch doctor really bloody carried on when he saw the crushed birdcage.

Sherm told how a couple of times that night he walked down the hall of Poppie's Guest House to Andrew Rouse's room, but just stood there before the door in the dark thinking about all their years together. Sherm went back to the porch and drank scotch. And then Sherm noticed that he could hear himself think—that the cicadas had turned off their racket for the first time since he arrived in Bali. And all he could think about was how he had to go back in and tell his best friend, Andrew Rouse, that it was all over—that Crown Royal Hotels had fired his ass. But Sherm, in his words, "never found the guts that night in Ubud to do the tough thing, the thing that needed to be done, the thing that should have been done much earlier."

So Sherm sat in a wicker chair and got drunk, and it started to rain. At first it was only a couple of scattered drops on the metal roof of Poppie's, then there were gusts of clattering drops, and then it was a torrential downpour. It wasn't the rainy season yet, but the street in front of the porch was suddenly a brown river. Sherm said he sat there thinking how they were going to need a damn boat, and then Sherm heard, over the roar of the rain, a woman screaming. The power went out right then in the whole village. The screaming was coming from inside Poppie's, and Sherm stumbled back inside and felt his way down the dark hall. He banged on the locked door and then put his shoulder hard against the door and the lock snapped off. It was pitch black in the room, and he felt his way to the bed, and then felt the shape of a foot. He ran his hands up Victoria's legs, felt her squirming on the bed. The kid Wayan arrived and held a kerosene lantern in the doorway, and Sherm could see Victoria. She was clutching her stomach and twisting her head back and forth in the pillow as she screamed.

Sherm held her glistening face in his two hands. The rain was so loud on the roof he had to yell at Wayan twice about finding a doctor, and the kid just looked at him and shook his head. Sherm said he looked down at Victoria and knew whatever the bloody hell her problem was, she had to see a real doctor pronto, and he picked her up and ran with her out to the jeep. When he got to the road he was sloshing up to his ankles in a river of mud. He got about two hundred yards down the road in his jeep before he slid off the road like he was on brown ice, and the jeep wedged at an angle against a banyan tree. Sherm stumbled with Victoria back up through the rain to Poppie's. Some of the men helped carry her back inside. The power blinked on for a moment and then went off again. In the flash of light he saw Victoria shivering from head to toe. He yelled for some blankets. In the hallway he could hear some of the men saying that the phone was still down.

It was then that Andrew Rouse and the *balian* ran into the

room. Both of them were covered with the dark brown mud, and all you could see were the whites of their eyes taking in the scene. The *balian* stood looking at Victoria with a distressed look on his face, but Andrew fell to his knees next to Victoria and started yelling over the pounding drum of the rain how sorry he was that he didn't stop her from carrying the birdcage—as if, Sherm said, the bloody birdcage had a damn thing to do with her being sick.

Sherm said the witch doctor and Andrew Rouse had a private conversation in the hallway—and then Sherm suddenly stopped telling all of us in the Rangoon bar his story, and just sat at the end of the bar tapping an empty shot glass. He didn't respond to any of the engineers yelling at him to go on, just sat there *tap, tap, tapping* his shot glass. The bartender tried to fill the glass and ended up nervously splashing scotch all over Sherm's hand. Then the bartender retreated out of the candlelight, and the engineers stopped yelling, and we listened to the rain pounding on the metal roof of the Rangoon bar.

Sherm finally started up again and said, so quietly that I had to repeat it for everyone, "The *balian* and Andrew took off into the rain, leaving me to take care of Victoria."

Sherm said he sat on the edge of the bed holding a damp towel to Victoria's head for the rest of the long night. He sent his men running down the road through the rain to get a doctor. When she groaned he held Victoria in his arms like she was his daughter, and during that night he realized that *he* would be to blame if this young woman died. I didn't understand why at the time, but let him go on with his story.

Sherm said that at dawn the pounding rain slacked off slightly, and little by little Victoria's fever started to break. It was still raining at noon, when Wayan brought in some food on a tray, and Victoria at this point was able to sit up and take a few mouthfuls of fruit. It was then that Sherm left her to go in search of the *balian* and Andrew.

Sherm suddenly stopped and looked around at us in the Rangoon bar with a look of disgust—as if he suspected the *balian* or Andrew was hidden among us engineers. He then closed his eyes and shaking his head told us he found the old Balinese bastard and Andrew out at the Monkey Forest Road site. They had rigged a tarp up in the trees over the site where Victoria had fallen on the birdcage with the ancestor spirits. Sherm absolutely didn't want to tell us what they had done. He kept shaking his head and looking into his empty shot glass. Turns out Andrew Rouse and the old *balian* had burned all the Crown Royal payroll for the month in a metal bucket. Millions of rupiah had gone up in smoke that night to appease the ancestors.

Sherm said he stood there in the jungle and told the two of them that Victoria was better, and said he just about wanted to cry when they hugged and grinned at the smoke coming from the old bucket.

Crown Royal Hotels wanted Andrew Rouse arrested by the Indonesian authorities. Sherm hung his head in the bar in Rangoon and told us how he hung up the phone and went to his old friend's room at Poppie's. From behind the thin door he could hear Andrew arguing with Victoria about how he wanted to stay in Ubud and study with the *balian*. Sherm didn't knock but went back to the porch and his bottle of scotch. He could still hear Victoria yelling at Andrew from the porch, so he walked down to the construction site. When he returned later that night the kid Wayan told him Victoria was gone in a jeep with her bags, and Mister Andrew had walked up the road to the *balian's* village. Later that night Andrew showed up out of the gloom of the road as Sherm sat drinking on the porch, and asked to be taken on as a common Balinese laborer. Sherm said he just couldn't bring himself to say no to his old friend.

Sherm perked up as he told us how he worked around the clock to get the construction project back on track. He set up gas-powered lamps and had three shifts of workers. Sherm said that if he saw some worker taking time off to pray he had the guy fired before he was up off his knees. He said one day they were putting up pillars made from tree trunks on the front porch of the new hotel, and some of the workers insisted the root ends of the tree trunks had to face the earth. Sherm said he didn't think twice, just fired the whole lot of them on the spot. One of the engineers asked the obvious question, and Sherm said, no, Andrew Rouse was not among those fired that day. He said Andrew worked harder than any native worker, and then every night went back up to the *balian*'s village to continue his "studies."

Sherm said that finally the Ubud Crown Royal Hotel's basic physical structures were finished, and it was time to start thatching all the roofs. It was on that day that Andrew Rouse came up to Sherm and spoke to him for the first time in weeks and said, "The *balian* says it is not a good day to begin thatching." Andrew had a big handful of the wild grass that they were going to use in the thatching, and started waving it in Sherm's face and rattling on and on about how wild grass is sacred to the Balinese, how it has a living spirit and needs to be honored.

It was at this point that Sherm stood up in that bar on that monsoon night in Rangoon. He turned to us engineers and said simply, "That was the last straw. I fired him. I finally fired my best friend, Andrew Rouse."

Sherm stood there and explained to us how the minute he uttered those magic words, "You're fired, Andrew," he saw his old friend crumble before his eyes. He said he understood right then that his friend's crazy delusions had been paper thin from the beginning and had only been allowed to survive and even thrive by Sherm's not taking a hard line. Sherm shook his square head and said remorsefully, "If I had just got my friend Andrew Rouse fired that first day he showed up in Bali and started sniffing the air and telling me it smelled like bloody perfume..."

Sherm went on to tell us how he left Bali for a few days and delivered Andrew Rouse back to his wife, and paid for Andrew's stay in the best psychiatric hospital in Toronto. He announced to us somewhat triumphantly that Andrew Rouse was today still on antidepressants, but working successfully as a consultant for a large commercial real estate development firm, and that he and his wife were very happy again and looking forward to his retirement. One of the engineers in the Rangoon bar yelled out, "Bloody good for them two!"

Right then the flickering fluorescent lights came back on in the bar. The lights seemed to surprise Sherm, and he looked at his watch and said he had to run. He reached in his pocket and took out his wallet. He looked in the wallet and then raised his face and smiled at me curiously, and reached into the wallet with his thumb and forefinger. He took out a small wadded clump of something and said to me it was some of the wild thatching grass Andrew Rouse had been waving in his face that day he had finally fired him. Sherm then nervously emptied the rest of his wallet onto the bar—enough money for us expatriates to drink for the rest of the night and through the next day. He shoved the empty wallet in his back pocket, and as he passed me he pressed the small clump of Balinese grass into my palm. Sherm looked me straight in the eyes as he closed my fingers firmly around the grass, and I swear he looked strangely relieved. Then he almost tripped over himself to get out of the bar and into the monsoon.

When he was gone I looked down at the grass in my hand. At first I thought nothing about it, but then I looked again and held the grass up to the fluorescent lights. The thing is this: *That clump of grass was still emerald green.* It was more than two years old and still hadn't dried out. You could put it to your nose and close your eyes and your head was filled with the scents of Bali. I showed it to the other engineers in the Rangoon bar that night, and they all cheered and toasted old Sherm for his "bloody good prank." One of the men took the grass, looked at it for a full minute, and then as he handed it back said, "He must of kept it in his refrigerator." I sat there in the bar looking down at the moist grass in my open palm, thinking how impossible it was still so fresh, and then remembered one of my last days on Bali, back at the close of my wandering twenties.

I had been surfing the pipes all day at Kuta. That night at a bar called the Topi Copi I met this woman who had until just recently been an ornithologist back in the States, working for Du Pont to prove a certain species of warblers was not in crisis. She told me how she had banded warblers in Massachusetts and then moved down to the Caribbean, and the first bird she captured on Tortola was the first bird she had banded up north. She added another red band on its leg, and when she went back up to New England a few months later, she was sitting at her kitchen table having a morning cup of coffee when she looked out the window at her bird feeder, and there was a doubly red-banded warbler cocking his head back and forth at her. She asked if I thought she was crazy for quitting her job, and I said at the time, "A lot of ornithologists probably use red bands."

Ceauşescu's Cat

I WILL TELL YOU about my twin brother Pavel.

It will take us back to Communist Romania in 1989. I had not seen my brother for almost a decade in this year, since the day he was thrown at age fifteen from the family house in Sibiu by our father, the colonel, for being a common thief. I agreed with this banishment at the time, and openly condemned my brother, Pavel, for bringing a stain on the good name of Popescu, and by extension, on Socialism.

As I said to you, my twin brother was missing without a word for ten years. So it was a great surprise when in 1989, during the dictator Ceauşescu's last months in power, my path again crossed that of Pavel. By this time I was not so righteous, and although I had all the right degrees with high marks in political philosophy from Sibiu University, was adrift and depressed as a sometime poet in Bucharest.

One day while trying to read my future in the water stains on the ceiling of my apartment on Galati Street, I heard the common phone ring out in the hallway. Although I had never sought the job, I was told to immediately report for a job interview with Laszlo Nagy of Romanian State Television (RTV). Like a combination of your Walter Cronkite and Johnny Carson, Laszlo Nagy was famous across Romania. His show was called *Hello Comrades!* Laszlo Nagy was the host, the director, the whole shooting match. His one show was all there was to watch on RTV in the afternoon.

In my interview for the job, Laszlo Nagy said he wanted to hire me because he was impressed by my poems he read in the dissident underground paper *Liberte.* I was of course surprised Nagy—or anyone at all other than its own handful of writers and artists—read *Liberte.* I asked Nagy if he was aware of the tepid anti-Ceauşescu nature of my poetry. Instead of answering my question, Nagy says he knows I feel *invisible,* and I am surprised he uses this precise word, as this *was* the exact word. The personal sense of invisibility at this time was so strong I was often angry at my reflection in a mirror, as if it was some sort of a cruel trick to torment me.

As I stood there unsure of what to do next, Laszlo Nagy barks at me to get the hell out of his office, go meet my cameraman, Gabor, and get to work making films. I thought—in dignity—I would walk right out of the RTV building, but instead went in search of this cameraman named Gabor.

Later on that first week I came to work at RTV, Ceauşescu's secret service killed people in France who had spoken against the Communist regime. And I said to Laszlo Nagy when I see him in the hallway: *will you report on this?*

He told me to come in his office. As I stood there Laszlo Nagy made a phone call and as I listened I knew it was the dictator Ceauşescu on the line. I was ashamed that I found this so exciting. And Laszlo Nagy gets off the phone and tells me to do a *happy hospital* or a *happy worker* story and this of course means we will ignore what is happening in Paris. So I say with sarcasm, *maybe I should report on a barber shop?* And Laszlo Nagy said, *Exactly.*

I knew I should refuse to be part of the Ceauşescu dictatorship's propaganda, but I did not refuse. I set out with Gabor to file my first "Commu-drama" for the State. A report on a barber shop, with me getting my face shaved in a chair in a row with eight others. And as we are all shaved we just talk like we are old friends. I asked stupid questions like: *why a haircut? for your wife? your lover?* And all this is on film, and at the end the shaving cream is gone and the bib and you see who the people were *really*.

Laszlo Nagy was smiling when he saw my first report—he finally said, laughing, "You idiot, Ovidiu. You have to have the words *Socialist* or *Ceauşescu* somewhere in your report. How can these people in the barber shop be so damn happy with no mention of *Socialism* or *Ceauşescu?*"

Of course, I knew what I had done, but I had to find some way to make this job palatable. And so my trick in my first reports is to rebel by what I do not say, by what is *missing*. And by some irony, when I do this small public rebellion, I find I am no longer as invisible *to myself*.

A few days later Laszlo Nagy has me on the assignment board for a report from the Sibiu Clothing Factory Number 3. I have to go talk to the female workers. The director of the factory comes out and he tells me he has prepared *a few good workers* and I say no, I want a few *bad* workers, his *worst workers*.

The director refuses, of course, and so I tell the director I will stand by the gates under the iron head of Comrade Lenin and talk to the workers when they come out. The director says, *you cannot just talk to any worker,* and I say as if innocent, *why not?*

The director tries to make the workers stay inside the gates until we go away. So we ask simple questions through the iron fence. In the beginning they see the RTV camera and they are scared, but then they start to *talk.*

I ask easy questions, like *how did you get to work?* One woman tells the camera her father-in-law escorted her, *as the streets were dangerous.* I ask another, *what will you cook your family for dinner?* She says with a smile, *meat.* All the women workers laugh, as all know this means she is *connected to the Party.* I go back to the RTV studio, put in this happy music, and make it more ironic.

Laszlo Nagy has already heard about me from the director of the clothing factory, and watches my report in his office for a half hour and then he turns it off and says without a smile, "Ovidiu, are you just fucking *crazy*?"

Yes! Yes! I *am* fucking crazy! Now you *see me.*

That very night I met Liana, a key player in this prodigal-son story. A spoiled girl, Liana was the daughter of the provincial governor of Transylvania. She comes up to me in a bar in Sibiu and tells me with big eyes how much she likes my work on RTV. She tells me I am becoming well known for my reports. This surprises me, as I have made so few reports, but it appeals to my vanity.

Liana is a college student and tells me she is having trouble in a course on Marx. It is easy to teach Liana the idiotic Marxist basics over wine. It was as if she already knew all about Marx, and about this I should have wondered more, as well as her tendency to look into my eyes and break into great tears.

And then a few days later (and before we have even kissed), Liana invites me to her father the governor's dacha in the Carpathian Mountains. She tells me this is not a traditional dacha, but a massive fifteenth-century castle. We go by a Dacia limousine and have a official motorcycle escort. In the back of the limousine we watch pirated Hollywood movies and drink imported scotch. Without telling Liana, I have invited twenty of my artist and unemployed friends from the underground paper *Liberte,* and they all show up at the dacha. To be an artist and unemployed in those days before the fall of Ceauşescu is like being a felon, and I expect we will all be thrown out by the governor, and I will be rescued from temptation.

So all these artists show up at the dacha, but the governor is strangely *not* furious and does not call the Securitate, but invites all to stay there with him for dinner. It was all very curious. I get drunk over dinner and I tell the governor about my Sibiu University graduate thesis, about how I proved Marxism does not exist, and how the professors all laughed at my work and scored me high. The governor laughs at this as freely as if we live in the West, and I put aside my suspicions about all this and think maybe he is not a bad guy. I ask him about the protests against Ceauşescu in Paris and he shook his head over the deaths as if these caused him personal pain.

The governor has flaming desserts brought out, and the best cognac. He toasts me in front of all my friends and says how *everyone knows me* and *how smart I am* and how I am *becoming famous* at RTV after only a few weeks. He says he knows I want to be Laszlo Nagy someday. He tells me how good it could be for me and his daughter Liana and he makes all my artist friends toast us as if she is my fiancée and Liana smiles at me as if this is true.

Later in the evening the governor is drunk and suddenly tells a story of how they hit a peasant when Liana was a little girl and took the peasant to the special Party hospital and only because of the top doctors the peasant lived. It is a story that drives off all my artist friends, and they are disgusted with me when I do not leave in protest. At this time I am fat with good food and drunk to the point of silliness and have set aside most of my disgust with the regime.

I pass out drunk in the castle's tower room on a feather bed. Sometime in the night Liana's father comes stomping up the stone stairs like the Ghost of Christmas Past. He is in black bikini briefs carrying a flashlight and tells me we will go for a drive. I think but do not say: *a midnight drive to knock down some peasants?*

So we roar drunkenly through dark Transylvanian towns in his black limousine. He keeps asking me about how I think it is in the West. All he wants to talk about on this drunken ride is the *West*.

At the end of this strange night ride, Liana's father pats my knee and tells me he is working to get me into the Romanian Communist Party. He tells me it is nirvana in the Party, and it is also a great honor. He then waves the scarecrow, tells me if I *do not* join the Party I will be hounded and the rest of my life will be miserable.

At dawn he drops me back off at his castle and drives off to govern Transylvania. I find Liana is naked in my feather bed in the tower. We make love like devils until she suddenly cries out in orgasm: *Pavel! Pavel! Pavel!*

It all suddenly makes crazy sense: I learn Liana was the lover of my twin brother Pavel and is pregnant. She will not have an abortion because she loves Pavel so much, and yet she tells me she will never see Pavel again. She explodes in sobs and I only learn that my brother—who as you will remember I have not seen since he was kicked out of the family home many years earlier—*has requested her to marry me,* and that she will do anything for him, including this. And this is why the governor wants me in the Party and to marry his daughter, as he accepts this crazy plan and agrees that I make better husband material than a common thief.

We drive around in her Volga for hours, and I learn little more to make sense of all this, as my brother Pavel has sworn her to secrecy. No one not in the Communist Party has a Volga and I see peasants and think how I might freely drive into them. Liana said finally: *we'll get married. I'll get you out and we'll go to live in France,* and I thought about this temptation for perhaps far too long and then said sadly, *no.*

"Why no?"

"Because you do not love me, but my brother the thief."

"Fuck you, Ovidiu. I did not offer to *love* you, only to *save* you."

"Perhaps I will get someday to the West," I said. "But I hope not from lies."

She tells me my brother Pavel did not anticipate I was so fierce as to refuse this offer. I say nothing as I am in a state of shock. Liana breaks the silence and asks out of the blue: *what will the West make of my fierceness if I go there?* Like gas in the air, it will dissipate until I disappear, she says. But I was not so fierce, and so in the end it is not *I* who will disappear in America.

———

I arrived at the RTV station later that afternoon in a snow-storm, and Laszlo Nagy said he would give me one more chance to do a propaganda film right. He sends me back out with the cameraman Gabor to film a traditional folk dance at Sibiu University.

On the way to the festival, as we go through this little town I see an old man shoveling the fresh snow and I say to Gabor, *stop the van.*

There is before us an old man in a blue coat. He has a big fur hat and a big shovel and he is this little man and he is going along shoveling snow and tossing it behind him, *right behind in the path where he has just shoveled.*

What he is doing makes no sense, says Gabor, when I tell him to film the shoveling old man.

"Yes," I say with a new sort of madness in my voice. "In our country it makes all the sense!"

Gabor is furious, tells me I am making a "Communist monster album," and I struggle with him for the movie camera in the street. He drops the movie camera and I pick it up and I film him cursing me as he walks away.

It is when I arrive back at the RTV station that I am told by Laszlo Nagy my brother Pavel was picked up by the Securitate and taken to my father's gulag. I ask Laszlo Nagy how he knows this, and he said he received a call from Tiberiu, and he says this as if Tiberiu is his oldest friend in the world.

Tiberiu is the Christian name of Liana's father, the provincial governor of Transylvania. I then see it was not an accident I—an invisible poet—was hired out of the blue a month earlier and given the chance for a career at RTV. Everything has been scripted, and I would be on easy street if I played my assigned part in this absurd Communist theater.

There is something important I have not told you. Our father, Gheorghe, was a colonel in the Romanian Army in the Internal Ministry, in charge of the political prisoners in the gulag at Sibiu. It is something I did not speak of after I finally moved out of the family house inside the gulag to matriculate at Sibiu University.

On this snowy day when I return to my parents' cement-block house in the gulag for the first time in a year, I find my mother is packing to leave my father, and she tells me my father had Pavel badly tortured on orders from Ceauşescu. I tell her they do not bother torturing common thieves, and my mother tells me angrily that I know nothing of the true nature of my brother, and that Pavel is a leader in the anti-Ceauşescu underground. She also tells me at length she is disgusted that I am working for Ceauşescu's RTV.

I have the movie camera on my shoulder, and I film my mother as she condemns me, and she tells me to put down the camera. I do not. I film her walking out the door with her one ancient suitcase.

An old guard by the name of Mihai, who played soccer with Pavel and I as boys in the gulag's prison yard, has tears in his eyes. After being refused in my request to see Pavel or my father, the colonel, I only film the slot window of the cell Mihai points to from the prison yard. When I yell encouragement to my brother Pavel, I am escorted at gunpoint from the grounds of the prison by Mihai.

You must understand this strange fact: We were not allowed to show cats on RTV. Ceauşescu hated with an insane passion the look of cats. And there was a cat on a wall of the prison yard as I was escorted out the prison gates by Mihai, and I filmed the cat looking down like a small god, and then I shot another cat I saw in an alley up the street, and I spend the afternoon as if in a trance filming all the cats in the streets of Sibiu and when I go back to RTV, I send the film directly to the censorship board without showing it to Laszlo Nagy.

Censorship cut the scene with the old man shoveling snow, and the scene with my mother cursing me, and the shot of my brother's cell window in the gulag, and the shots of a dozen cats in the streets of Sibiu, but they strangely leave fifteen seconds of footage of the first cat I filmed—the one that looked down like a small god when I was escorted from the gulag—and when I see this cat on RTV that evening, I am so happy I get roaring drunk.

Then I go drunk as Bacchus back to the RTV station and I go in to see Laszlo Nagy in his office. He just got off the phone with Ceauşescu, who is crazy mad about seeing the cat on RTV.

"I am a cat," I proclaim to Laszlo Nagy before he has a chance to say a word to me. "Unlike you, I am a cat."

Laszlo Nagy just stares at me and then says calmly, "Securitate has orders from Ceauşescu to pick you up this evening at your apartment, but I am sure you will not be there. You may well be a cat, but unlike your brother Pavel, you are not a crazy fool."

Laszlo Nagy was right. I was not in my apartment that night. I escaped into Bulgaria and then into Greece inside a tanker truck filled with cooking oil. For eight hours I sloshed up to my neck, and at the borders I slid under the greasy oil when the border guards look into the tanker. I held my breath for maybe four minutes until the tanker top clanks shut again. My brother Pavel and I always had this one odd thing in common besides our looks: Since childhood we could hold our breath for many minutes.

For two months I am in Athens, translating for refugees at a Baptist mission. Unlike for my brother Pavel, for me school

133

was always an easy pleasure, and I spoke five languages. One day the Baptists tell me there is a new Romanian who refuses to say two words at a time but happens to look identical to me. Pavel refuses to answer questions about his arrest, torture, or escape from our father's gulag. Pavel only tells me: Liana was shot dead by the Bulgarian border guards. He is without emotion in the telling, and then will speak no more.

My brother and I are accepted to go to America. We are invited to see the American ambassador because we are political refugees, and that week Americans were proud of doing things for political refugees and are having a party at the embassy to celebrate their good works. We are dressed up by the Baptists as we are Exhibit A, and so we go to the fancy party.

I see Pavel at the party slipping silverware into his pockets and even up his sleeves as he ate the shrimp. He stands with his arms crossed when he meets the ambassador and does not shake hands, as he has too much silverware up his sleeves. The ambassador looks like the Disney creature Goofy. He is talking to a group telling them how difficult is the English language. He said, "For example, I might say: I send my son *abroad*, or I send my son *a broad*." He laughs hard and sprays the refugees with bits of shrimp.

Pavel is hit by shrimp bits and calls the ambassador, in Romanian, *a stupid pig*. All the refugees laugh, and I tell the ambassador Pavel translated his "broad" joke. The ambassador throws his arm around Pavel and so Pavel says to him in Romanian, "Get your arm off me, you stupid pig."

One of the Romanian refugees says, "Peeg, Peeg."

"Pig?" said the beaming ambassador. "Pig?"

"Pavel is a farmer," I said. "He wants to farm *pigs* in America."

Pig is the magic word for the ambassador. The ambassador

has a *big thing* for pigs. He has a silver pig on his tie. He takes Pavel out on the veranda and the two smoke cigars. I have since learned that Americans have *big things* for this or that thing that makes no sense.

A man in a ugly suit comes over and says hello in Romanian. He tells me he knows all about my brief career at RTV. He asks if I will work for Radio Free Europe. He tells me I will have a good salary, a checkbook for expenses, and the chance to do good for Romanians. Pavel comes over as I talk to the man in the ugly suit. Pavel's arms are still crossed. He motions to the suit. "Who is this asshole?"

"He wants me to work for Radio Free Europe."

"You will do it," said Pavel. "You will stop being such a stupid brother."

"I want to be free of all politics," I said. "Radio Free Europe is more disgusting propaganda."

"You are a child," said Pavel. "Forget politics. Take the money." With a mouthful of shrimp, Pavel turned to the suit and said, "What's the pay?"

"More than the silver up your sleeves," said the suit.

Pavel shrugs and walks off toward the champagne. I did not expect my brother to speak against politics, and with so much intensity about money.

As we are leaving the party, Pavel motions to the walls of the embassy and says with the first hint of a smile I have seen on his face since his arrival in Athens, "In America I'll be a millionaire thief and have a big house like this one."

There are many refugees I see at the Baptist mission in Athens. But I see not only people coming from the East and going to the West, but also people *coming back* from the West. I meet a number of these strange people. A Romanian returning said in

America they were like ghosts. He told me with anger I should never go to America, that I will disappear.

One afternoon a week before before we left on a Air France flight for America, I got a call on the Hotel Perseus phone. When I picked up the phone in the hallway I hear the voice of my old RTV boss Laszlo Nagy. I said the obvious question, "How do you know where I am?"

There was a deep silence, and Nagy finally said, "Ovidiu, what do you think?

"I think it must be Securitate."

"Damn right."

"They made you make this call. So they are listening."

"Yes."

"Why'd they make you call me?"

"You are not planning anything stupid, Ovidiu?"

"What do you mean?"

"Just don't do anything stupid."

"Where did you get this crazy idea?

"Stay out of politics."

"You must know I want nothing now but to stay out of politics."

Laszlo Nagy hung up. It was a crazy phone call.

A few days later Ceauşescu came to Athens. I hung out the window of the Hotel Perseus and watched the motorcade as it races down the narrow empty boulevard.

My brother was in the dark of our hotel room watching a TV he had stolen and I said that the devil had just passed in his motorcade. Pavel did not move his eyes from the TV. This was strange because I expected him to show some sign of hatred toward Ceauşescu.

———

The American embassy told us we were going to be sent to the city of Reno. I asked why and was told: *it's a roulette wheel*. Tomorrow it might be Cleveland, and the next day, Seattle. There was no sense to it.

The heat was like getting hit over the head with a baseball bat. It was 120 degrees in Reno. We are put in this hotel in a disgusting section of Reno and it is like a United Nations slum. All the immigrants want to go right to a casino to gamble their free money. That night Pavel and I see all the free shows and gamble like the other idiots.

In the morning, after the casinos all night, my brother and I go to the supermarket. All the food is so fake, all the vegetables are waxed so horribly. This is a disgusting forgery of real food. In Romania there were shortages, but we go to the farmers' market every day and the food is all organic and there are no pesticides because the farmers are too poor for these. Then Pavel tries to bargain at the supermarket, and there are problems.

The supermarket manager calls the cops when Pavel in outrage throws the wax cucumbers, and we hear the siren and must run. We have only been in America fifteen hours. Pavel stops at the back door of a house of cement block. This ugly house was the mirror of our childhood home in the gulag. Pavel rings the bell and then breaks a small window in the door with his elbow and we go inside.

And then time slows down. Pavel makes Turkish coffees and we sit at the kitchen table and talk of little things. It is as if we are again at the family table back in Sibiu in the years before Pavel was thrown out. Into this quiet talk between two brothers, Pavel said suddenly, "You have a handicap."

"What is this handicap?"

"Come on," said Pavel. "You know you are a cripple."

"Tell me why I am a cripple."

"Where is your hunger for money?"

"Once it seems you cared about more than money."

"This was before prison."

One night a few weeks later when Pavel is out working as a thief, two FBI men come by the Reno apartment. These two guys are seven feet tall with thick necks and look like bodyguards. They are very slick and at first I wondered if they were from the Securitate. Sort of irkingly polite, but you know they are SOBs under the suits.

They asked about the crazy call from Laszlo Nagy I got a week before we left Athens. I said, "How did you know about this call?"

"Ovidiu, are you working for Greek Securitate?"

"Why would you trust me if I say no?"

"You're pretty clever, Ovidiu."

"So how did you know about this call from Laszlo Nagy?"

"Were you involved in a plot to kill Ceaușescu when he came to Greece?"

I tell them they are crazy. I wanted nothing to do with politics when I escape from Romania. I only wanted this vague idea I had of freedom as a sort of *anonymity*. They ask me to explain this, and I try to distinguish for them between the freedom of anonymity and the terror of enforced *invisibility*.

As we talk—and I am very upset you understand to learn all they have on me in their files here in the land of freedom— I finally learn from the FBI that my brother Pavel called the Romanian Securitate during our final days in Greece and said: *either you let certain political friends out of prison or Ceaușescu will die when he comes here to Greece*. And Pavel told them I was in on the plot in case they thought he was unable to pull it off himself.

One evening after we have been in America a month, Pavel comes by the pool as I sit there torching my flesh in the crazy desert sun. The pool has too little chlorine and is feverish with algae. Pavel wears a black silk suit with gold chains he thought from TV was worn by the American criminal class. He insists I admire his wallet, fat with twenties and fifties. He throws some bills in my lap and tells me I must stop being a cripple.

Pavel at this time liked the song by the Talking Heads: *Don't touch me, I'm a real live wire, Psychokiller, Qu'est-ce que c'est?* He dances to this song and dives in his criminal clothes into the pool. I watched him swimming at the bottom of the pool in his suit like a shark. He stayed down for almost five minutes, and it is as if he is saying to me: *here is proof no matter how much I change I am still your brother.*

Pavel stole a convertible Cutlass Supreme a few nights later. We go out and drive in the desert and then he pulls over at the side of the road. Pavel was rarely in contemplation but the air is thick with the fumes from his ruminations. He is drinking heavily and finally I say, "You are making much money as a thief, Pavel."

"More than ever in life."

"So why this sadness?"

"I steal and no one takes notice."

"Who do you want to take notice?"

"I don't know this."

"So what is the problem?"

"It is too much like a job."

And that night in the desert I learn that back in Romania,

all that my brother Pavel and his band of thieves stole from the very beginning went to make a pool of money for the overthrow of Ceauşescu.

The Romanian Revolution then began in the city of Timisoara. Pavel showed little interest as I listened on CNN to the few reports. The revolution was started by a priest who must have been a friend of Pavel's. I assumed some of the dead were once friends of my brother, but Pavel would not talk to me of the revolution.

And then the dictator Ceauşescu is gone from power. He and his wife are executed. At the time I tell this news to Pavel he shows no outward reaction but begins going inward, he never leaves his bed, and then he starts going out at night and coming back drunk and stupid. He clearly no longer has the dream of becoming a millionaire American thief.

One night Pavel does not go out to drink. He sits naked in the kitchen listening to idiotic top-forty radio with his arms hugging a stolen boom box. I turn off the boom box and ask Pavel about the threat to kill Ceauşescu when he came to Greece. Pavel says he knows nothing about it. I ask him if he is lying and I am not sure he is lying. I suddenly do not even recognize his face. It is now a American face, a face of the corpses in the streets of Reno.

I want to bring back Pavel's old face, the one I knew from childhood. One Sunday afternoon Pavel sits in the apartment with a six of Budweiser, trying to watch a SuperBowl game like all the other Americans. I come out of my bedroom and stare at him. It is as if he has a cancer.

I go back inside the stifling bedroom and sweat as I fail to write poems. Pavel finally leaves the football and beer and comes into the bedroom and bugs me to go somewhere. He shows me a brochure for a tourist place outside of Reno called the High Noon Ranch.

I see his face then, the shining face he had when my brother was a boy.

"Let's go," he says, "it's a place that has *cowboys.*" Because of his enthusiasm for cowboys, I for a moment see this as a novel idea and agree.

It is then, as I agree to go with Pavel, I receive a mysterious phone call from my old cameraman Gabor and learn that Laszlo Nagy barricaded himself in the RTV studio during the riots in Timisoara and then when Ceauşescu's soldiers break down the door he shot himself.

It is a mystery when I heard Laszlo Nagy was dead, but then it all makes more sense when Gabor tells me about the cats. Laszlo Nagy showed my cats film during the riots in Timisoara over and over on RTV. A dozen cats on a repeat loop. I hang up the phone and suddenly I want to get out of the disgusting apartment too. As I leave the apartment I can see before my eyes the face of Laszlo Nagy as clear as if in a photograph. I said out loud to this vision of his face, *I see you now, Laszlo Nagy.*

High Noon Ranch is an oasis thirty miles outside of Reno, one of those kitschy tourist landmarks only the American West can produce so well. As we drive there for the first time Pavel talks about the uprising, and Pavel tells me that he should have been there in Timisoara for the rebellion. I ask him again if he threatened to kill Ceauşescu when he came to Greece. Pavel said nothing for miles, and then as we pulled into the High Noon Ranch, Pavel said, "The one who called Securitate with this threat was dying at that time."

———

The High Noon Ranch had a pond with some ducks, a museum with some of the first gambling tables in Nevada, and a zoo. There are these pigs there at the zoo and Pavel and I talked about the American ambassador to Greece's crazy thing for pigs and Pavel said he should have known then.

"Known what?" I said.

He looked at me like I was stupid, and then said as we watch the cowboy actors come out of a trailer for another shootout that the America he always dreamed about had *cowboys*. He tells me this is the happiest he has been since we left Romania, seeing the *cowboys*.

I said, "You idiot, Pavel. They are just actors. They mean nothing."

The actors fake a Old West shootout in the streets of this fake Western town and an actor falls down and spills some ketchup into the street. Tourists are getting into it, and Pavel moves closer to the fake action.

After a few minutes I look at the tourists and suddenly I cannot pick out Pavel. I walk around to the other side of the crowd. I cannot pick out his face among all the tourist faces. It is as if he has disappeared. I give up looking for him and go inside the museum to stare with other idiot tourists at old slot machines.

Two cigarettes later and I go out and wander through tourists and still can't find Pavel. He's got to be somewhere there, and I think maybe he's in this fake Abraham Lincoln log cabin that is made of plastic. Pavel is not in the plastic log cabin. He is nowhere. As missing as rain in this desert.

I find steps that lead out into the desert beyond a barbed-wire fence and so I head out into the desert. A guard rides up on a broken old horse and says, "You can't go out there. Snakes. One bite and you're a dead man."

The fake cowboy calls on a walkie-talkie, and then there are all these fake cowboys circling around me on sad broken horses, and then they all trot off in search of Pavel. I stay there until midnight and then I go back and sit in the slum apartment in Reno. The next day I go to the police station. What the police are saying to me is, *Pavel is just another missing guy.*

After he is missing forty-eight hours we finally go in a police helicopter and fly over the desert at the High Noon Ranch. The cop asks again some of the same questions. "Maybe someone abducted him?"

"No one saw any struggle in the parking lot."

"Maybe he hitched a ride from the ranch?"

"Then why would he leave his visa and money in the car?"

"Do you think he killed himself?"

"Where then did he hide his own body?"

It is totally and absolutely flat for miles in all directions from the High Noon Ranch. The cop looks at all this terrible flatness and says, "Right about that. Hard to hide a plug nickel out here."

For months afterward Pavel came to me in dreams and with his index finger touched a glowing red spot like a ruby to the pale skin of my chest. This spooked me.

One night when I am awoken by this spooking dream of my twin brother, I go over to our neighbor Marta's apartment. Pavel used to sleep with Marta before he was too down even for sex. Marta is asleep on her couch in front of MTV. I go out on her porch and drink from a bottle of scotch and look at the sky and then I see a satellite. It is moving like a red ruby across the desert sky. *You are watching me, you bastards!* I give them the finger, but it is a stupid, useless gesture.

Marta comes out on the porch. I ask her, "What can I do about a satellite?"

"What do you mean, *do*?"

"It is a checkmate here in America."

"You're fucking crazy, Ovidiu."

If I am now crazy, Marta is crazy also. She is sure it is an *alien spaceship* that has abducted my brother. She also suggests that maybe if not aliens, then the *mob*, or perhaps the *Dominicans* or *Colombians* or *CIA*. I shake my head at all this insanity. Marta took a toke from her joint. It is at this moment that I decide I must do something to give sense.

I go back to my apartment and get all Pavel's clothes and put them in a big green garbage bag. As I am walking to Pavel's car with this bag, Marta runs out and says she wants to come with me.

I drive back to the desert at the High Noon Ranch, and in the light of the headlights I dig a hole to bury Pavel's clothes out there. I find myself telling Marta with enthusiasm about the day I filmed all the cats and got one on the air at RTV. Marta can make nothing of this and tells me I spend too much time alone in my own head.

I dropped the shovel and shook the garbage bag of Pavel's clothes into the hole. With my hands I covered them with the warm desert sand. As we walked to the car Marta asked me about the purple scars on Pavel's thighs and testicles. I told her that they were marks from the day my brother died back in Romania. She does not understand why I have said my brother died back in Romania.

Driving back with Marta from the desert that night after burying my brother's clothes, there is a white cat lying as if dead on the highway's yellow lines.

We are miles from Reno and in nature there are no house cats in the desert. Marta and I stare at the cat in the headlights. I get out of the car and feel a rapid heartbeat under the thin ribs and carry the cat back to the car and insist to Marta, *this cat must live!* I am absolutely crazy about it.

We take the cat to a twenty-four-hour emergency room. The doctor wears the blue-striped Adidas nylon running pants favored by undercover Securitate agents. He says like there is no doubt I have a terminal disease, "It is just a dead cat." The way he says it is to tell me: *It means nothing.*

I ask the doctor for a slip of paper and a pencil. I write a first line for a poem: *It is just a dead cat.*

On the way home Marta insists the same as the doctor: *It is just a dead cat.* She also tells me it smells bad. I am very angry and yank the cat by the tail from the plastic bag as we drive into Reno and swing it like a lasso around the inside of the car. Marta is crying, and she grabs the cat when the tail breaks and throws it out the window.

I stop the car. We are in downtown Reno and the cars honk. I get out and walk back to this cat. I kneel down and hold the cat in my arms, and I know a small poem for my brother:

> *It is a dead cat,*
> *but not Ceauşescu's Cat.*
> *Here it is just a dead cat.*

The Mayor of St. John

IT WAS A MYSTERY to most St. Johnians why the newly elected governor of the Virgin Islands, Samuel Moses, had appointed a substitute history teacher at the Julius E. Sprauve Elementary School mayor of the island. For many days there was no other question from the West Indians slapping dominoes at the taxi stand in Cruz Bay to the whites throwing horseshoes at Skinny Legs Grill in Coral Bay. Only Sebastian Vye, his mother Miss Ellie Vye of John's Folly, Governor Samuel Moses, and the governor's legitimate son, the developer Victor Moses, knew Sebastian Vye was the "outside" son of the new governor.

Sebastian Vye himself, when told by his mother Miss Ellie that he was the new mayor, as he looked through his collection of artifacts on the wooden floor of their old-style West Indian home in John's Folly, was as surprised as anyone on the island. Licking a shard of a slave's pottery to test its antiquity, he told Miss Ellie in his nervous stutter that he had no interest in becoming the mayor of anything.

Miss Ellie sighed heavily as she sat in the single chair in the room. She looked up at a lizard on the rotting beams of the ceiling and listened to the soft patter of a wisp of rain on the rusted steel roof and said with a smile on her plump ebony face one word to her forty-two-year-old bachelor son: *Eustacia*.

Sebastian put the shard of pottery down on the tarp and closed his eyes. Miss Ellie leaned forward in her chair with effort and said, "You de mayor, you save de donkeys. You save de donkeys, dat pretty girl you been giving de eye year by year, Eustacia January, she then your own girl."

Sebastian Vye had no idea what his mother Miss Ellie meant about the donkeys, but he understood that as mayor he might suddenly be in a position esteemed enough to satisfy the family of Eustacia January. Her father, Liston January, had in the new Moses administration been reappointed head of WAPA, the Water and Power Authority for the three Virgin Islands. Other than the governorship, there was no more powerful position in the islands than controller of the tens of millions of federal dollars flowing through WAPA. Sebastian knew his mother had forced Governor Moses to make him the mayor, but he knew better than to ask the St. John matriarch for the details. When his mother heaved herself from the chair and left the room, he slipped the framed photo of Eustacia January from under his pillow. He had blown the photo up ten years earlier from her graduation photo from the Sprauve School and had laid his head down on his pillow delicately every night since. He found an old bent nail and a rock, and for the first time in a decade, he hung her up over their small dining room table, exposing the sweet but frightened face of the former Miss St. John Carnival 1989 to the tropical elements.

Miss Ellie stuck her head back into the room as he sat looking up at Eustacia January in her carnival crown.

"I goin' say this once, Sebastian," said Miss Ellie. "But dat girl Eustacia January, she always for you, she *waitin'* for you all these years. She waitin' for you to *do somethin'*."

The red-roofed Battery sits on a small peninsula of land in Cruz Bay Harbor, the main entrance port to St. John from St. Thomas. Built of painstakingly squared-off brain coral by slaves in the early 1800s, it had an elaborate white iron balustrade surrounding the second-story veranda, from which the mayor can survey the harbor.

Cruz Bay Harbor was too small now for its moored yachts, commercial barges, and ferry traffic; the ferries wove too quickly between the dozens of yachts, some of which were the homes of sailors known as liveaboards. In his first week in the Battery, Sebastian had been presented with twelve complaints from irate white liveaboard sailors of near misses by the ferries. Sebastian treated each sailor with West Indian civility and sat behind his desk in jacket and tie and slacks taking down in his patient script pages of the sailors' often drunken rants, which usually jumped quickly off from the original incident and extended into a monologue on the ineffectuality of the West Indian government.

Sebastian put down his pen after the EMT and liveaboard sailor Kent Lyle left his office after complaining about a near miss of his yacht *Anchorage* at midnight by the ferry *Bomba Challenger*, shook the knots from his fingers, and sniffed the sailor's body odor crowding his office. He slipped his notes into a file labeled INCIDENTS IN CRUZ BAY HARBOR, which he was preparing to show to the Department of Planning and Natural Resources on St. Thomas. He took a handkerchief from his pocket and dabbed at the perspiration beading on his forehead. The phone rang. It was his father, Governor Moses, calling for the first time since taking office two weeks earlier.

"Dat you, Sebastian?"

Sebastian could barely hear Governor Moses over the roar of a helicopter outside the Battery.

"Sebastian!" yelled Governor Moses. "You look outside, dat me in de helicopter."

Walking to the open door to his office, Sebastian waved to the thin black face staring down at him from the passenger seat of a sleek black Narcotic Strike Force helicopter hovering over Cruz Bay Harbor.

"You listen, now, Sebastian," said Governor Moses. "I on my way to Coral Bay for a meeting. We goin' talk hurricanes. You still there, boy?"

"I here."

"Sebastian, I ask you, what you doing about dem donkeys?"

"Dem donkeys?"

"Dem wild donkeys dat eating all de orchids."

"De orchids?"

"Don't monkey me, boy. Dat's a big problem, all dem wild donkeys. Dey eating all de orchids of dem rich whites you got over dere in Chocolate Hole. Dey complain to me, dey complain to Washington, den Washington call me with de problem. Now I calling you, Sebastian. What you doin' about dem donkeys?"

There was static on the line, and Sebastian watched his father pass over Cruz Bay Harbor shaking a hand at Sebastian from the helicopter. The line was dead, and Sebastian cradled the heavy old receiver and walked out on the veranda of the Battery.

Just that morning, Sebastian had received an outraged letter from an old white man, Langley Cunningham of Chocolate Hole, complete with photos of him standing among the devastated ornamental orchids around his villa. Sebastian had admired the colors of the few surviving orchids, which were not native to St. John and could not have survived in his youth when roof-captured fresh water was at a premium and the multimillion-dollar desalination plant had not afforded the luxury of drip irrigation, and started a file he labeled DONKEYS AND ORNAMENTAL ORCHIDS. He wondered if he could obtain a few orchids from Langley Cunningham to lay in Eustacia January's Jeep someday if she left it in the parking lot near the customs house when she took her monthly trip to visit relatives on Tortola. Sebastian Vye laughed out loud from the balcony of the Battery as he pictured the delight on the face of Eustacia January, who loved brilliant colors, always had a brilliant red hibiscus blossom in her hair like the old-style West Indian women.

The mayor shook his head and went back into his office and returned with an antique Danish spyglass and raised it to his left eye. Sebastian instinctively avoided looking at the villas strewn across the hillsides of the island of St. Thomas, two miles away across the sparkling aquamarine channel; he turned the spyglass slowly, searching for the deserted island of Little St. James. Sebastian had built, in the last ten years, an elaborate vision that he and Eustacia January would marry and move out to Little St. James and live an old-fashioned, simple West Indian life. Now, as the mayor located Little St. James with the spyglass, he watched as a crane on a barge lifted pallets of concrete forms onto a cleared brown swathe. Sebastian turned the spyglass quickly away from the swinging pallets and ran his eye along the dark lines of the reef in the passage between St. John and St. Thomas. A cargo barge pushing a wall of sparkling foamed sea before it, steamed into his line of vision and out again. Something on the barge caught his eye, and he swung the spyglass back, but there was nothing to see but a small wall of water pushed before what he now saw was the *P'Ti Blue* barge.

The mayor stood on the veranda of the Battery with the spyglass dangling in his hand by his side. He closed his eyes as a breeze worked through the somber heat. He remembered a day nineteen years earlier in the cool of the small rain forest at the top of Bordeaux Mountain. He was walking down from the rain forest, moving down a gut following the trickle of water among the ferns. Soon the gut dried up and he continued down the dried riverbed until his path crossed that of the Reef Bay trail. He heard children screaming ahead of him on the trail. He ran ahead and around two bends he came upon nine-year-old Eustacia January and five or six other schoolgirls in the plaid skirts and white blouses of the Sprauve School, standing like small black statues in the green shadows. Ahead of them a boar snarled and kicked at the trail. Sebastian pushed his way past the girls. The boar raised its head. Sebastian Vye raised his arms at his side and involuntarily flapped them like a frigate bird and strange hooting sounds passed from his lips. He hooted and flapped and the boar stared, tilting his bristled snout from side to side, and then turned and crashed away through the bush. When Sebastian turned back to the girls, little Eustacia January threw herself into his arms. He carried her back up the trail, and she clung to him all the way back by Jeep to the January home on Moorehead Point, where her mother, Yolanda, had to pull her away.

As forty-two-year-old Sebastian stood on the veranda of the Battery he still felt Eustacia January's nine-year-old arms around his chest. Eustacia January had grown up to be the prettiest and shyest West Indian girl on St. John. She was elected Miss St. John Carnival 1989. During the talent portion of the carnival contest, with St. John's entire West Indian community looking up at the stage built on the Sprauve School ball field, she froze and only hummed along with the sound track from the Big Baron's calypso song "We Run T'ings," but was still awarded the crown. She went away to the University of Pennsylvania for college but was back a month later and didn't come out of her grandmother's Moorehead Point home for three months. Then she founded the Animal Care Corps, and began transporting dogs and cats by ferry to St. Thomas, where Dr. Kingston, a West Indian veterinarian, spayed and neutered them for free. Her goal was to reduce the rising population of starving wild pets left behind or lost to the bush by whites. Sebastian saw her on occasion at dawn, standing at the end of the Cruz Bay ferry dock with a cat or dog in a plastic carrying case. Once she turned and smiled shyly, but Sebastian Vye's feet were lead.

The mayor opened his eyes and looked out to sea from the veranda of the Battery. The barge *P'Ti Blue* slowed down for the Gallows Point reef at the entrance to Cruz Bay, fell back and settled, the rush of foam lost under the bow. The barges brought Jeeps and building supplies hourly to the island from St. Thomas. Sand, bricks, cement blocks, plywood, steel, tropical hardwoods, I-beams piled onto St. John's small industrial dock. The barges had been beach landing craft during World War II. Marines once stormed onto beaches from the barges, then called LTVs. Now the barges were painted the colors of candy.

Something was moving around on the *P'Ti Blue*'s deck. The mayor squinted and leaned forward over the iron balustrade. The deck of the *P'Ti Blue* was alive with donkeys. Donkeys covered the otherwise empty barge deck. The *P'Ti Blue* didn't bear off to the industrial dock but headed straight for the rocky shore of the Battery. Sebastian Vye dropped the antique Danish spy-glass in surprise; it rolled under the iron balustrade, fell to the rocks below, bounced into the shallow water. One of the donkeys looked up from the bow of the *P'Ti Blue* at the mayor and brayed loudly.

The barge *P'Ti Blue* pushed aside the stern of a small sailboat as it made its way toward Cruz Bay beach in a narrow and shallow slot along the rocky shore of the Battery. There was just enough room for the barge to pass. Sebastian Vye ran down the stone stairs and out of the Battery, ran huffing with his tie flapping over his shoulder down Waterfront Street, past the health clinic, where he was followed by the curious eyes of the EMT Kent Lyle sipping a Pepsi while sitting on the bumper of the ambulance. The mayor could hear the hydraulic front gate of the *P'Ti Blue* barge lowering as he ran toward Cruz Bay beach. He ran around the clapboard taxi stand and found the *P'Ti Blue*'s front ramp half-down. Idle taxi drivers looked over from their dominoes game on the bandstand in Cruz Bay Park. Edgar Marsh, a second cousin of Sebastian Vye, held a domino aloft. Behind the descending ramp, the donkeys were leaping to get out of the barge. A couple of shadowed faces were in the dark square pilothouse of the *P'Ti Blue,* and Sebastian waved urgently. A single donkey ran up the angled ramp and flew toward the shore, four legs flailing in the air. The donkey thrashed ashore kicking up water and looked back from the beach at the other donkeys still on the barge. Sebastian Vye stood by Miss Gertrude's safari taxi, with its longhorn cattle horns mounted on the hood, and waved his arms at the shadows in the pilothouse.

The donkeys still on the *P'Ti Blue* were all braying, and the ramp fell with a whine and *clunk* into the sand of the shoreline, and the donkeys raced out as one. The donkeys fell over each other up the short beach, over the stone wall, slipped between the rows of safari taxis and charged into Cruz Bay Park.

The nearby ferry *Bomba Challenger* had recently off-loaded a few hundred tourists. There were still a dozen or so tourists in the park not yet herded on the safari buses for the ride to Trunk Bay Beach in the National Park. These tourists scattered as the donkeys charged in a circle. Heads aloft, ears pinned back, the donkeys charged as if in the center ring of a circus. One donkey leapt up on the bandstand. It crashed through the card table set up by the taxi drivers for dominoes. Sebastian Vye ran after the donkeys as they brayed and circled the park. A white woman tripped and fell, and a donkey skidded to a halt before her and raised himself up on his back feet, as if in victory.

Sebastian Vye stopped dead in his tracks when he saw Lieutenant Jeffreys running into the park from Sparky's T-shirt shop. Lieutenant Jeffreys had for the last ten years worked as an elite Narcotics Strike Force officer on St. Thomas. A few weeks earlier, a real estate developer from Miami had been found executed by a single pistol shot to the back of the head in his St. Thomas waterfront condominium. The real estate agent was in a legal wrangle over the last of the Jeffreys family land in Charlotte Amalie. Most of downtown Charlotte Amalie, the capital and harbor of the island of St. Thomas, had once belonged to the Jeffreys family. Lieutenant Jeffreys was sent to St. John, where it was assumed he could lie low until the murder was forgotten. Instead, he spent his days stepping out of the bush at the side of St. John's roads, flagging down whites at gunpoint, searching their cars, ticketing them for minor infractions. Now Lieutenant Jeffreys was in front of Sparky's T-Shirt Shack in a firing squat, his pistol trained on a donkey rearing up at one end of the park. Lieutenant Jeffreys fired, and the donkey fell dead, nose first, into the dirt.

Sebastian Vye saw Eustacia January running down the street toward the park, and he looked quickly back at Lieutenant Jeffreys, who was marching in a half squat across the park, his pistol trained on a second donkey as it spun on its hind legs and kicked the air. Sebastian looked back at Eustacia January running in her bare feet, her sweet round face flushed. She was pointing to Sebastian Vye as she ran toward the donkey aimed at by Lieutenant Jeffreys. Sebastian Vye turned and ran toward the rearing donkey, placed himself in Lieutenant Jeffreys' line of fire. He heard the officer yell at him. The donkey's hoofs flashed in front of his face. As he waved his arms like a frigate bird in front of the rearing donkey and started to turn back to look for Eustacia, something cracked him in the back of the head.

Sebastian Vye awoke on a gurney in the hallway of the Morris DeCastro Clinic. He was looking up at an enlarged photo of his father, Governor Moses, smiling down from behind the nurses' desk. Kent Lyle, the bearded EMT, was looking down intently into his eyes.

"How many fingers?" said Lyle.

"Fingers?" said the mayor.

Kent Lyle had no fingers out and laughed at his joke. "You're going to be OK, Mayor Vye. He got you pretty good. I had to put in ten stitches. We were out of sutures, so I used some red and green thread. Kids around here like the rasta colors. How about you?"

"Donkey kicked me?"

Kent Lyle took two steps backward in mock surprise. "The donkey? Donkey didn't get you, Mayor Vye. That coked-up cop, Lieutenant Jeffreys, he pistol-whipped you good when you got in the way of his shot. Surprised he didn't plug you. If you were white, you'd be dead right now."

"Coke?" said the mayor.

Kent Lyle hopped up on the counter of the nurses' station. He said, "You sure are out of the loop for the mayor. Jeffreys is lit up day and night. He'll kill someone here, but they won't put him away until he does, and even then it's doubtful. Too many people in high places making too much money on the stuff." Lyle took out a cigarette, lit it, and pointed to Governor Moses' photo on the wall. "Like Governor Moses over there."

Sebastian Vye's head throbbed. He had never actually been a patient in the Morris DeCastro Clinic, although he knew they were always short of supplies and knew right now the only real doctor was in a psychiatric hospital in the States. He turned to Kent Lyle and said, "What about the donkeys?"

Kent took a drag on his cigarette. "Donkeys took off for Bordeaux Mountain."

Sebastian Vye waved his hand toward Kent Lyle. "No, *why* did someone bring them to St. John?"

Kent Lyle whistled and said, "You kidding me, Mayor Vye? You don't know?"

"No," said the mayor. "I'm sorry."

The pain drummed louder in the back of his skull as the mayor shifted his head on the gurney. Kent Lyle took a deep breath and said in a single long rush, "The governor's son, Victor Moses—you know him. He's been over here every week, taking out Eustacia January. But the word is he's made slow progress. And then Eustacia January heard earlier this week, like everyone else on St. John but you, Mayor Vye, that Governor Moses plans to *do something* about the donkeys over here, because all the rich white villa owners over in Chocolate Hole are losing their ornamental plants and they gave the new governor a lot of money in his campaign. Anyway, you know how crazy Eustacia January is about animals. So Victor Moses promised to save St. John's donkeys for her, and seeing how crazy she is about the donkeys, he decided to barge some more over for her. So that's what he did this morning, unloaded all those donkeys from the *P'Ti Blue*. But then there was that coked-up Lieutenant Jeffreys to mess up his plan."

Kent Lyle took a deep breath and said, "So that's the story." Lyle jumped off the nurses' station, came over, and placed a finger on Sebastian Vye's forehead. In the midst of a now-blinding headache Sebastian Vye heard Kent Lyle say, "It isn't all bad news, Mayor Vye. You got a big kiss from Eustacia January." Lyle went to the wall near the nurses' station, took a small mirror off the wall. He came back and held it over the mayor's head. There was a perfect pair of red lips painted on his black forehead. The mayor sucked in a breath. He took the mirror in his hands, stared at the perfect round lips bright on his forehead, brought the mirror closer, and the throbbing pain in his head grew smaller until it drifted away.

The mayor marched with a spark in his step out the swinging doors of the emergency entrance to the DeCastro Clinic with his fingertips beneath the kiss on his forehead. From within the clinic he heard Kent Lyle calling after him about a concussion. It was a Caribbean day of such splendor the mayor wanted to raise his arms and cry out, and spotting old Miss Hendrick, one of the tellers at the Chase Bank, walking across the customs house parking lot, he cupped his hands—as Miss Hendrick was slightly deaf—and called out, "Marvelous day, Miss Hendrick!"

Miss Hendrick's son, Melvin, was one of the five young crack dealers who in the last few months had taken up evening residency outside the Chase Bank in the center of Cruz Bay, and recently Melvin had been found bound, beaten up, and burned by cigarettes behind the Moravian Church in Coral Bay. Miss Hendrick turned and looked hard at the mayor, and Sebastian Vye slowly lowered the hand that was raised in greeting.

Sebastian Vye was checked in his ebullience only for a moment, however, and strolled toward the Post Office. He forgot about old Miss Hendrick, forgot about his natural reserve, and touched his forehead beneath the blazoned kiss again gently, with two fingers. Henrietta Parsons, a transplanted Manhattan real estate agent, came out of the Post Office loaded down with packages. The mayor jogged over and took four or five off her hands, walked with her to her car. She glanced a few times at his forehead. The mayor beamed up at the sky and said, "Isn't it a good day, Miss Parsons?"

Henrietta Parsons jiggled her keys in her hands in front of her Jeep. Her lawyers had recently worked their way through a tangle of disputed West Indian family claims to a hundred acres on the east end of St. John and a road had been bulldozed, and Parsons Real Estate was now offering waterfront half-acre lots on a gated and guarded compound for four hundred thousand dollars each, and she was preoccupied by forty million dollars. Everything had to be *perfect* if the sales were to proceed as planned, and she had heard the local St. John newspaper, the *Tradewinds*, was planning a front-page story on the *donkey problem* soon, and it was just the sort of thing that would send her stateside investors skittering off to St. Barts or Antigua or Tortola. Henrietta Parsons jiggled her keys again as the mayor held her packages. She opened and closed her mouth a few times and then said, "Did you know you have ketchup on your forehead, Mayor Vye?"

Sebastian Vye nodded as if he had been waiting for her to notice and said, "It's lipstick."

"Lipstick?"

Sebastian Vye nodded again and decided to tell her the whole story, but as soon as the mayor said the word "donkey" Henrietta Parsons cut him off and said, "We all have been given to understand by Governor Moses that you plan to do something about the donkeys, Mayor Vye."

Henrietta Parsons gave the mayor such a severe look that he forgot for a moment what he wanted to tell her, and his hand rose weakly toward his forehead.

"Do you want a tissue to wipe that off your forehead?" said Henrietta Parsons.

"No," said the mayor. "No, thank you."

Henrietta Parsons looked at him oddly for a moment, then shrugged and said, "What are you doing right now, Mayor?"

The mayor shook his head. He felt a throbbing returning in his skull. He couldn't remember why he had strode so firmly out of the DeCastro Clinic. He took a quick glance at the blue sky. Henrietta Parsons waved a hand before his eyes and said, "Are you there, Mayor Vye?"

The mayor focused on Henrietta Parsons, who said as if there were to be no arguing, "I have an idea, Mayor Vye. Why don't you come with me up to Chocolate Hole? I can show you just what sort of terrific damage these donkeys are causing us."

Over Sebastian Vye's mild protestations, he was strapped

firmly into the passenger seat of the Jeep by Henrietta Parsons. She squealed out of the parking lot and roared up Centerline Road. Some West Indian schoolgirls looked over from the playground of the Sprauve Elementary School. The mayor was pushed back in his seat as Henrietta gunned past a safari taxi driven by Nathan Penn around a blind corner in Estate Enighed. The Jeep bounded over the top of the hill at Jacob's Ladder, and there was Lieutenant Jeffreys holding his gun at his side by the edge of the road. Sebastian Vye saw Lieutenant Jeffreys lean over and spit on the ground as the Jeep passed him. Henrietta Parsons seemed not to see the police officer; she was beeping hard and waving furiously at a Jeep coming up toward her. She stopped in the middle of the road and Sebastian Vye looked over at Langley Cunningham, the old man who had written him a letter that morning about the donkeys and his orchids.

"I've taken the mayor hostage," said Henrietta Parsons.

Langley Cunningham looked over from beneath two heavy gray beetle brows. He seemed to be examining Sebastian Vye from his position bent over his Jeep's wheel. "I see you have, indeed," said Langley Cunningham. "Has he cut himself? What's that on his forehead?"

"Lipstick," said Henrietta Parsons. "Langley, why don't you follow us? You can help me educate the mayor about our concerns."

Langley Cunningham slapped his steering wheel. "He needs to eradicate them. Shoot them. Poison them. Kill them. I don't care what Vye does. Damn pests."

The mayor's headache had returned in force, along with a dizziness, and he rocked from side to side as Henrietta Parsons swerved through the newly paved roads of Chocolate Hole. Along the way she picked up Barnard Hoyt, who also agreed to come along. He followed Langley Cunningham in his Land Rover.

The three vehicles slipped down the steep driveway to Henrietta Parsons's villa. Flowers surrounded them in a rock garden on all sides as they passed through an electric gate. Bougainvillea, hibiscus, frangipani, and orchids blooming in disorder. Henrietta Parsons led them up through the rock garden till they came to an area where the flowers were trampled and there was nothing but short frayed stalks close to the ground. Henrietta Parsons pointed to a knocked-down fence, and she bent down and cupped the remaining stalks and said, "My pretty babies. Oh, my pretty babies."

She looked up at Sebastian Vye and said harshly, "Do you believe us now? Do you see, Mayor Vye? Something has got to be done."

Langley Cunningham and Barnard Hoyt joined Henrietta Parsons in staring at Sebastian Vye, who bent over and picked up a stray orange petal. Henrietta Parsons shared a look with the two men, and led the mayor across the steep hillside. The mayor looked down at black plastic pipe snaking everywhere around his feet; he looked above and saw the concrete cistern built into the hillside to water the plants in the dry season. The water was bought from the desalination plant at Moorehead Point and trucked up once every few weeks during the dry season. Henrietta stopped and pointed down to a series of posts lying on their sides, tied together by barbed wire.

"Be careful," said Henrietta. "The top wire still has elec tricity running through it."

Hoyt took off his cap, wiped his forehead and said, "Fast as we put up the fences, they just push them down."

The three of them stared at the fence, and then Henrietta led them down to the villa. It was a three-story steel and glass building. Everything within the villa was white. The pool was built at the cliff side so the water fell over the edge as if falling into the Caribbean Sea hundreds of feet below. Sebastian Vye had never been in one of the million-dollar villas that were slowly covering the island. He turned around, and there was Eulinda Harvey, his third cousin, in a white-and-black maid's uniform, with a platter of drinks.

Henrietta Parsons took a drink from the tray and as she handed it to the mayor said, "St. John isn't big enough for both of us anymore. The donkeys will have to go. You see that, don't you, Mayor Vye?"

"What's that smudge on your forehead, Mayor Vye?" said Hoyt.

"Lipstick," said Henrietta Parsons.

There was a thrashing sound from inside the villa, and Henrietta put down her drink at the edge of the pool and went inside. Sebastian Vye looked out at the island of Little St. James. The barge was still out there, dropping concrete forms. There was a scream from the house, and the three men ran inside. A young donkey was standing in the doorway of the villa, looking curiously from side to side. Henrietta Parsons had taken refuge behind her white counter and was waving her hands at the donkey and saying, "Shoo. Shoo. Bad donkey."

Sebastian went up to the donkey, took some nuts out of a white ceramic bowl on the counter, held them out. The men were yelling behind him, asking Henrietta if she had a gun. The donkey stuck his nose in the mayor's palm and he pulled his hand just out of reach and led the donkey out the villa's door. He led the donkey up the stone steps through the flowers, opened the gate and closed it behind the donkey, and led him down the dirt road. When he looked back once, Hoyt was standing in the driveway with a shotgun held before his chest.

The donkey followed him out to Gifft Hill Road, where he rubbed the young donkey's nose and swatted him on the behind, sending him toward Reef Bay, and then the mayor hitched a ride back to town in the back of Herman James' empty safari taxi. Herman was playing a tape of the St. John All-Stars in the cab, a steel pan group made up of island children. The music took Sebastian Vye back to his childhood in the late 1950s. There were only a dozen eccentric whites on the island, and they all lived at Gallows Point and said *Good morning* and *Good evening*, as was the West Indian custom. He remembered there were no cars on St. John in those days. There was only a donkey path up and over Bordeaux Mountain to distant Coral Bay, and at the top of the mountain you were in a rain forest where it was so cold you shivered and the mist was so thick it was like standing in a cloud. Sebastian Vye had a donkey he raised named Shego, and he would ride her up to the rain forest at the top of Bordeaux Mountain and sit in the cold in a trance and listen to the orchestra of yellow-and-green tree frogs for hours barely breathing, for if he moved at all they stopped their ancient song.

Sebastian Vye climbed out of the safari taxi at the Chase Bank and walked down toward Cruz Bay Park. He stopped for a moment to speak to Pastor Sovingreen of the West Indian Emmaus Moravian church. The pastor reached out with a handkerchief, and before Sebastian could argue he had wiped away the smudged remains of Eustacia January's kiss from his forehead. When Sebastian realized what the pastor had done, he felt his knees go soft. His palms flew to his forehead, and he walked off without another word.

He walked with his hands on his forehead. Some tourists passed by and snickered, and their children raised their hands to their foreheads. An island dog came toward him and stopped in the road. It was a yellow-and-black mutt, with matted hair and ribs showing. He wagged his tail weakly at Sebastian Vye and then came forward with his head bowed and sat down before the mayor. The mayor looked down at him, and he took his hands from his forehead and scratched the dog behind the ears. The dog stood up and wagged his tail. The mayor walked into Cruz Bay Park and sat down on a bench and closed his eyes. The park was empty except for the taxi drivers slapping dominoes near the bandstand. In a few minutes it would be full again, with a flood of tourists returning from Trunk Bay.

The mayor heard footsteps. He felt someone sitting next to him on the bench, smelled sweat and cologne. When he opened his eyes slightly he saw a pistol being flipped around on a black finger. He saw the black arm was thickly muscled. He felt goose bumps rise on his skin.

"Dis island too small for all," said Lieutenant Jeffreys.

The mayor closed his eyes. After a while he heard Jeffreys sucking his teeth loudly. When the mayor opened his eyes, Lieutenant Jeffreys was gone. A taxi full of tourists arrived, the women in bikinis, the men pink chested and slathered with white lotion.

The mayor sat as taxi after taxi brought hundreds of tourists into Cruz Bay Park. Some went down the street to the T-shirt shops, others milled in the park, waiting for the next ferry. Sebastian Vye touched his forehead and stood up and walked out of the park through the tourists. He heard something behind him and turned to see the island dog was following, wagging his tail. The mayor walked out of the town of Cruz Bay along the shoreline toward Frank Bay beach. He climbed up a narrow road and stopped to pick some hibiscus flowers of the most delicate pink hue, and again he touched his forehead with two fingers.

He stood at the edge of Frank Bay beach and looked out toward Moorehead Point, a short, bulbed peninsula of land. The Mooreheads had sold their half of the point for the new desalination plant. The larger portion still belonged to the January family. There were two new white government Jeeps in the driveway up to the new double-floored cinder-block and shuttered home. The mayor approached the gate with the hibiscus blossoms clutched in his shaking hand. As was the old Virgin Islands custom, he called out loudly, *"Inside!"* from the gate, and Eustacia January's grandmother Miss Gertrude came to the half door and waved him up the rocky and barren dirt path. He walked up through their herd of goats.

The mayor sat in the dark living room with a glass of lemonade, and one of three little girls, Eustacia's nieces, handed him one of Miss Gertrude's homemade sugar candies. The darkness of the slat-shuttered West Indian house struck him for a moment as backward in comparison to Henrietta Parsons's open-walled glass villa, then he was enveloped in the shadowed quiet and took a long sip of lemonade.

Miss Gertrude looked at the hibiscus blossoms in Sebastian Vye's hand. After a long silence she said, "What take so long, Sebastian Vye?"

Sebastian lowered his head and looked down at the hibiscus blossoms in his hand. "She waitin' for you all these years," continued Miss Gertrude, shaking her gray-haired head. "She waitin' and waitin' for you, and Victor Moses, dat man come sniffin' 'round dis house every day now. Dat Victor Moses tell her all de time you and his fada, Governor Moses, got somethin' bad cooked up for de donkeys on dis island. I tell her, you crazy girl, dat Sebastian Vye, he not hurt de fly on de donkey's head."

Sebastian took a deep breath. The little girls looked from their grandmother to Sebastian. Miss Gertrude took a sip of lemonade and said, "I tell her, you wait, dat Sebastian Vye, he a good man and he come. He old-style St. Johnian: he polite, he decent, and he care for all de little t'ings. I say, Eustacia, ain't no men no more on dis island like dat Sebastian Vye. All de men here, dey lose all dere sense and drink and do de drugs, or dey runnin' after de big white money like dat Victor Moses." Miss Gertrude sucked her teeth and pushed herself from her chair, came over and took Sebastian Vye's hand, and said, "She comin' back on de nine ferry from St. Thomas. You see her, den you tell her what you come here to say."

Miss Gertrude went into the kitchen to warm a bowl of goat soup for the mayor. When Miss Gertrude hobbled back into the living room with the bowl and a Heineken, Sebastian Vye was gone, and the little girls were each holding a handful of hibiscus blossoms, rubbing their foreheads with two fingers, and giggling.

The next morning Sebastian Vye awoke with a hangover. He had drunk a quarter of a bottle of Cruzan rum as he sat in his bed looking at his photo of Eustacia January. He had planned to drink the entire bottle but had passed out too soon. He had gone to the Cruz Bay dock to meet the nine ferry in his Sunday suit. At the entrance to the old dock was a small red-lettered sign announcing the construction of a new two-million-dollar federally funded ferry dock for St. John. The dock was to be built by Victor Moses Construction. Liston January, Eustacia January's father and the head of the Water and Power Authority, was listed as a member of the project's advisory board. Governor Moses's photo and enlarged signature adorned the bottom of the sign. Sebastian Vye had stood before the sign for a long time, and then turned and gone to Joe's Package and bought the bottle of Cruzan rum and hitched his way home.

He stood up from his bed and was struck by the stillness. No thrushie was calling, no rooster was crowing, no cicadas humming in the heat. He looked out through the slats, and the sky was a dark, heavy blue. Sebastian Vye closed his eyes and felt a hurricane brewing, but by the time he arrived at the Battery, he had forgotten his premonition. He sat for a moment at his desk, went out on the balcony, and looked over at Little St. James. He could see a bulldozer scraping the tiny island. The mayor left his office and got in his white government Jeep. He sped up Lind Point and then down North Shore Road through the National Park. He passed the entrance to Caneel Bay Resort without glancing at the manicured grounds, but his hands squeezed the steering wheel. He felt faint as he passed Hawksnest Bay, the parking lot full of Suzuki rental jeeps and safari taxis, the West Indian park employees picking garbage off the sand in the shade of the trees.

The mayor squealed up the switchbacks of Dead Man's Hill, and as he sped past Cinnamon Bay, the mayor knew his destination. He stopped at the tourist overlook at Maho Bay, got out of the Jeep. He looked down at the blue-green crescent of Maho Bay. On the end of the beach near him was a small green house behind a barbed-wire fence. As he looked down he watched two white tourists walking along the beach toward the house. The mayor stared at the green house, wondered if she was home; and then from the bushes she emerged, the "madwoman of Maho," waving her machete at the tourists and screaming. The tiny old West Indian woman remained there screaming and waving her machete long after the tourists had retreated.

The mayor walked down the road. He caught his breath as he stood hidden behind a tree looking toward Estelle Ditliff's house. Standing in the backyard next to Estelle Ditliff was Eustacia January. She had one leg raised under her and was bobbing her head in imitation of a great blue heron for her great-aunt. She stood on one foot and bobbed her head, and then she suddenly turned her head and seemed to spot Sebastian Vye. She smiled in his direction, and he ran back up the road to his Jeep and sat in the Jeep trying to think of ways to save the donkeys for Eustacia January.

When he raised his head from the steering wheel the sun was setting, and as the mayor drove back along North Shore to Cruz Bay the horizon over St. Thomas was washed by fiery stripes. He rounded the last corner on winding North Shore Road and looked down upon Cruz Bay from Lind Point. He drove slowly down the steep incline and came upon the first dead donkey in the road at the foot of the hill. He got out and went to the donkey; the headlights of his car made the dead donkey's eyes glow amber. The donkey was shot in the ear. From downtown Cruz Bay he heard the echo of a shot, and then another. Sebastian ran toward the shots. He heard one closer, near the ferry dock, and he ran past the post office and the Morris DeCastro Clinic. Sebastian came upon the second donkey by the phone near Cruz Bay Beach. The phone was off the hook and it dangled near the donkey's still-quivering ear.

The mayor wondered what had caused the donkeys to run back into Cruz Bay from the bush. It was as if they wanted to take the ferry off the island. He heard footsteps and saw the ambulance driver, Kent Lyle, run up and put his hand on the dying donkey's ears. Lyle stood and ran off toward the echoing sounds of another two shots. He turned halfway across Cruz Bay Park and yelled back, "It's Lieutenant Jeffreys."

The mayor ran after Kent Lyle across the park. There was a dead donkey bleeding from a gut wound onto the gravel in front of the Back Yard bar, one shot through the eye in front of Chase Bank, and another thrashing its legs in front of Cruz Bay Realty. There were two white men bent over the donkey. One wearing a Panama hat turned, and Barnard Hoyt gave him an odd look. The mayor nodded, and Hoyt said, "Here I thought you people couldn't do anything right."

The mayor turned away and raised both hands to his forehead, looked back at Barnard Hoyt once, and started running down the road back toward the National Park. Hoyt looked after him. The mayor ran with his hands on his forehead, and as he ran he saw a Jeep's lights coming down from Lind Point and he raised his hands and gestured as if to push it back up the hill. His lungs burned as he saw the Jeep slow to a halt before the donkey In the road. He saw the Jeep door open as he ran, saw a figure bent over the donkey in the headlights, and as the mayor ran up and yelled, *"Eustacia!"*, she bent and kissed the dead donkey's head. He stood gasping for breath before her and when she raised her face to him he cried out.

Sebastian Vye was found later that night at the villa of Henrietta Parsons in Chocolate Hole. Every flower in her garden had been hacked to the earth. He was lying naked and filthy with a machete by his side, rubbing a handful of flower petals to his forehead.

He is no longer the mayor of the tiny Caribbean island of St. John.

He is obese now and his belly lolls over the gunnel of the filthy pants cut raggedly off at his knees and held up by a length of line given by a yachtsman who said he was tired of looking at the crack of his black ass. He sports a tattered vest, and has a long feather hanging from his right ear and a sun-faded Minnesota Vikings cap backward on his shaved skull.

He doesn't talk to tourists, but will carry luggage with a shuffling gait and an obsolete smile for a dollar a bag. He buys cold Heinekens with the crumpled cash and sits in the shade under the one palm tree not torn down to build the massive new St. John dock, and as he waits for the next ferry from St. Thomas he picks at the corns on his bare feet and is no more present than the panting, flea-plagued island dog by his side, until memories of Eustacia January rise like the late-afternoon moon in an otherwise baby blue Caribbean sky—then his eyes flare as bright and round as those of any tourist stepping off the dock toward his tiny island.

A Predictable Nightmare
on the Eve of the Stock Market
First Breaking 6,000

SHE BOARDED in Tucson without a ticket. She left her Filo-fax in a phone booth when she dashed out and boarded the train. There was no cash in the Filofax left behind, her Fleet checking account was frozen so the ATM card was useless, and the dozen credit cards from Visa and American Express down to Bloomingdale's were all overextended and canceled.

The conductor kicked her off the train at El Paso. Melanie Applebee watched the Amtrak train grind away from the asphalt platform. She wore a damp black Chanel suit, and around her long neck was wrapped a double strand of large pearls. She flipped her bleached-blond hair with the back of her hand. The train was lost around a slow curve and she briefly ran the tips of her fingers over the pearls. She swiveled suddenly around to look at the red-brick, high-steepled El Paso station with a delighted look on her face, as if she heard an old friend call out her name.

Melanie Applebee stared at the public phone in the cavern of the El Paso train station and touched the pearls at her neck. The pearls were strangely warm. In the first few weeks after the firing she had raised her hands to remove the pearls a few times a day, but she always stopped and her hands froze, as if someone had suddenly grabbed her wrists. At first it had felt odd—to wear the pearls in the shower, or to bed—but a few months after her firing the large pearls had become natural, as if she had entered the world with the pearls circling her neck.

Her breath whistled in and out past her perfect white teeth, over her tiny pink tongue. Her teeth had been straightened and whitened at her own expense while she was in business school at Stanford; it was this tongue that, almost of its own accord, had formed the words to tell Don Firt her suspicions over lunch at the Four Seasons, that Henry Smyth was trading on inside information. Don Firt put her in a cab and sent her home after the lunch, his bald pink head shaking.

The few items on her desk arrived by messenger a few hours later, and the messenger told her to turn in her ID. After that it was as if an iron curtain had fallen between her and the company. She sent out résumés, but no consulting or investment firm offered even an informational interview; someone— probably Henry Smyth—was blackballing her on references. Without solid references from her sole employer since Stanford, no respectable firm or headhunter would even talk to her. She had an inexplicable eight-year hole on her résumé.

She had been celibate for more than four years, had long operated as if her work were her sole mission. Her closest relationships were with the Greek men who worked the deli five stories beneath her apartment at the corner of Seventy-ninth and Madison. She would take her two coffees large and black at 5:30 sharp every weekday morning and most Saturdays, and with a few fierce strides cross the sidewalk from the deli and disappear into a waiting limousine.

She had nearly maxed out her credit cards before she was fired, and in the following six months quickly ran through most of her small cash savings and her unemployment compensation. She slept during the day and awoke sweating and shaking late every afternoon.

Melanie was finally invited by letter to come for an interview at a consulting firm in Tucson. She didn't recall sending them a résumé, but could vaguely picture their small ad in the Sunday *New York Times*. The firm specialized in the retirement community construction industry. The firm sent her only a one-way ticket. She assumed it was a mistake, but was too fatigued to call to have it corrected. It took an enormous effort to shower, pack a bag, and get to Kennedy for the American Airlines flight to Tucson. As the taxi drove to Kennedy, she realized she had left her overnight bag back on her bed.

When she arrived by taxi at the office of the consulting firm, A. R. Bernard, Inc., the U.S. Treasury Service was wrapping the building in yellow tape. It was a late casualty of the savings and loan crisis. She got out of the taxi and walked around the office building. The taxi driver called to her, and when she didn't respond he shrugged and burned rubber. She found it difficult to organize her thoughts when she turned and saw the taxi going away. At a phone outside a nearby gas station the operator connected her to a taxi service, after first suggesting she sounded like she was in trouble and needed the police to take her home. She told the taxi driver to take her to the airport. When told there was no seat that evening on a flight to New York City, she made a morning reservation for the next day, and took a shuttle bus to the nearby Camino Real Motel.

She missed her flight the next day. She had fallen asleep without asking for a wake-up call. She went in the bathroom and by accident dropped her green-tinted contacts down the sink. She looked steadily at her own brown eyes in the bathroom mirror for the first time since Stanford. She leaned toward the mirror and stared angrily at the black roots beneath her blond hair. At some point she went out and returned with a bottle of Absolut.

Planes vibrated the paperboard walls and blotted out the televised sounds of the world economy as it winged upward. On day four, as she stared at the Sony through her toes, Melanie closed her eyes and had a vision of herself seated in a shadowy Four Seasons, blurting out to Firt about Smyth's insider trading, and in the vision she was dressed in a golden Valentino dress, and the pearls around her neck were oddly aglow, and the only apparent light in the restaurant.

The Camino Real Motel's manager, a fat man with a Fu Manchu, came to her door at noon on the fifth day and told Melanie her fifth credit card had failed and she had an hour to vacate or he was calling the police. She yelled at him in her ludicrously high-pitched voice, and he grabbed her by the wrist, pulled her from the room, and then flung her briefcase over the balcony and into the pool. She slapped him, and he picked her up by her thin, muscular arms and tossed her over the railing and into the pool. She swam around, tried to gather together the soggy sheets of her résumé as the ink melted off into the overchlorinated water.

She drip-dried as she made her way from the Camino Real

Motel by foot back to the airport, and then randomly climbed on a shuttle bus, which deposited her at the Tucson train station. When she was unable to produce a ticket or a credit card on the train, the conductor threw her off at the El Paso station, and looked down at her as if she were insane as the train pulled away.

And so she stood by the public phone in the cavern of the El Paso train station, fingering the warm pearls around her neck.

Melanie Applebee walked through the El Paso station and stepped outside onto a brilliant white stone plaza.

Her heel caught and broke off in a crack as she walked briskly across the plaza, and she stumbled and fell. She lay face down, her knees and hands burning. She pushed herself up and kicked off the other black Ferragamo shoe, sent it arcing across the plaza, looked at the gravel embedded in her bleeding palms. A Latino with an eye sealed shut as if by a hot poker retrieved the shoe and tried to hand it to her, saying something in Spanish.

"He said you shouldn't throw it away, Señora. Such a pretty shoe is very expensive," said another old Latino man, walking over from a bench under a tree. Melanie said nothing and the man added, "You need help, Señora?"

Melanie Applebee glared and said sharply, "I don't need anyone's help."

She shielded her eyes from the sun and looked around the plaza at the Americana Museum, the Performing Arts Center, a tourist information booth, and in front of the booth, a trolley. She was pulled toward it, saw the faded sign on the tourist information booth: THE EL PASO–JUÁREZ TROLLEY CO.—RIDE THE BORDER JUMPER. There was a long line of tourists in front of the ticket booth. She stood in the line for ten minutes before she looked down and was surprised to discover she wore no shoes, and then she remembered she also had no money.

A mariachi band passed in front of the line of tourists. When they passed, she looked up from picking the gravel from her palms and saw the teenage boy. He looked like he was in the line of tourists for the Americana Museum, but he was watching her. She felt faint and sat down on a bench. He walked over and sat down next to her. He said nothing, but she glanced at his sharp, slightly chinless profile, and for a moment she couldn't place him; but then she realized he could have been Henry Smyth's son. At first she felt angry, as if it were Smyth himself, and then she laughed, a high-pitched, hysterical laugh that she tried to swallow off. The boy heard it—he couldn't have been more than fourteen—and turned and smiled at her, with Smyth's same cocky attitude.

"My husband forgot to pick me up," said Melanie.

"You're a tourist," he said, and pointing to her ringless finger, added, "You're not married."

"You're right," said Melanie, smoothing her skirt against her knees. She was strangely blushing at her own lies. The boy looked over at her and held out a ticket with a picture of the green-and-white rubber-wheeled trolley. "I'll sell you one for half price," said the boy.

Melanie looked for a long time at the ticket and finally said, "I don't have any money."

The boy turned to her then, opened his mouth; she saw the teeth going in every direction, as her own had once. After making it out of Des Moines and through Yale and the Stanford School of Business, she had tried to erase from her memory everything previous to her first day of consulting work. Her real name was actually not Applebee, but the Greek Apostolokis.

She had cut her parents out of her life during business school, when they had refused to evolve into the WASP parents of her imagination, or even call her by her new name.

The boy nudged her and when she focused on him said, as if he had thought the matter over, "You sound like a little girl, like my sister, you know that?"

"I've always had this high-pitched voice," said Melanie. "I've tried to do something about it, but I can't seem to help it. It's one thing I'm stuck with, I guess."

The boy suddenly handed over the trolley ticket. She looked at his face, saw something vaguely like Smyth's look when he closed a deal, but ignored it and took the ticket. She stood and walked across the plaza and was on the packed trolley before she realized she hadn't even thanked the boy. She turned to lean out the window to wave at him, but he was by her side. The trolley lurched forward and she fell, and he grabbed her by the arm. His grip was surprisingly strong.

"My name is Kyle," he said. "Or Carlos, if we're over the border in Juárez. Kyle in El Paso or Carlos in Juárez. You should of thanked me for that ticket."

He still gripped her arm, and Melanie said, "I'm sorry. It's been a difficult day."

Kyle nodded and said, "What are you doing in El Paso?"

"I'm looking for a job."

"Get a job. Then you can get some shoes."

Melanie looked down at her feet, closed her eyes, and seemed to force out after a struggle for the proper words, "And what do you do, Kyle?"

Kyle let got of her arm, ran his hand over his buzz-cut yellow hair. "Me? I'm a *fronterizo*. A border rat, you know? A little of this, a little of that. You cut the best deal in the market. It's *una lucha* every day, you know?"

"*Una lucha?*"

Kyle shook his head, took her by the arm again. "I got to help you, little sister. You know shit. Coyotes around here eat you alive." Kyle tightened his fingers and held her arm and said, "*Una lucha,* a battle."

Melanie looked down at her stockinged feet. Kyle pointed in the direction of a strip mall, where a billboard proclaimed *Oshkosh y Mucho Mas* and said, "Hey, you want to go legit, *princesa,* there are jobs all over El Paso. That KFC over there, I know they're hiring."

Melanie Applebee raised her head quickly, looked over at Kyle in surprise. Kyle caught her look, said angrily, "So you're not looking to work at KFC? It too good for a pretty blond Anglo like you?"

"I have an MBA."

"You got an MBA, but no shoes." He grinned, let go of her arm again. The trolley stopped. He said slowly, "Hey, I'm a big asshole. I know businessmen. They'll hire you. A blond Anglo like you with a MBA, no problem. *Electromecanicos.* Semiconductors. You know anything about them?"

Melanie struggled again for words and then found herself saying slowly, "All companies are fundamentally the same."

The boy looked at her closely, shrugged, and said, "You want me to find you a job right now?" He pulled at her arm urgently, as if she had challenged him to find her a job. The trolley was still stopped; the conductor was telling a tourist avocados must have their seeds removed to be brought back into the United States. Kyle was pulling her off the trolley, singing about *electromecanicos* and big dollars.

Kyle talked nonstop as he walked her along the streets. He told her, laughing, about how across the border in Juárez he'd heard the Mexicans yelling at an American couple, "Want to get married?" When they said they were married, the Mexicans yelled, "Want a divorce?"

They passed a cinder-block church with green plastic windows. He sang what he called a *corrido* called "*Muerte del Burro*," about a criminal who steals from the Mexicans crossing the Rio Grande. The criminal was burned at the stake. As he burned, the criminal cried out his innocence. Kyle said, "He's so stupid, he doesn't even know what he's doing to his people is so bad."

Every time she hesitated in following him, Kyle rhapsodized about the high pay at his uncle's semiconductor factory, the need for Anglos in the front office. They were in a grass lot now, walking along a path between two empty fake-adobe houses.

Kyle stopped in the path. At his feet was a large black bug. He tapped it with his boot toe. "*Pinacate* beetle," said Kyle. "Tap it and it gives off this killer smell."

"I just need a job," said Melanie.

Kyle raised his face, said, "Give me twenty bucks for the trolley ticket. Ten bucks, plus interest."

"I told you, I don't have any money," said Melanie, raising her palms. "You said it was free."

Kyle spit and said, "Nothing's free here. Give me the pearls."

He wrestled her to the ground face down, drove her upper body into the dirt, grabbed at the pearls. She screamed and caught him in the stomach with an elbow. She wrapped her hands around the pearls around her neck, curled into a fetal position. He kicked her hard in the kidney. She heard him running away. From the edge of the lot he yelled back, as her back spasmed, "You're such a crazy stupid bitch, you'd not even get a job at KFC!"

Melanie Applebee lay in the grass of the empty lot, one hand on the pearls still around her neck. There were monsoon thunderheads above in the pink sky. In the distance she could hear the cars on the I-10 expressway.

As the shadows lengthened she remembered her first big presentation at White/Weld. Ten men from Merck Pharmaceuticals. She reached into her briefcase to begin her presentation, whipped out her folder, and a tampon dislodged, jumped from her briefcase, and tap-danced down the long mahogany table. All ten men looked at it, and there was a long silence until she said, "We are here, gentlemen, to stop your company's hemorrhaging." The men were quiet, and then laughed. Smyth told her later she had not only saved her job, but won the account. He called her a genius.

She stood in the empty lot, swaying slightly, and smoothed her skirt over and over. Melanie Applebee walked in the pink glow of the late afternoon, repeating Stanford Business School Professor Steven Galamudi's axiom: *every macroproblem is solvable by a multitude of microdecisions.* Bats flitted past her face. A black child biked past her and spit a wad of bubblegum at her.

She wandered down empty streets lined with concrete-block buildings bearing signs for ZAPATOS SEMINUEVOS, MAGNETOTECH, KWON TOK ENTERPRISES. Melanie wandered from street to street until she found herself staring up at a lit red-and-white sign. Up on the sign Colonel Sanders was looking back at her from across the small square. She stood looking into the Colonel's glowing plastic eyes, rimmed with black glasses. Melanie was suddenly, in her mind, inside a limousine. When she worked late, the company limousine took her home. They always passed a busy KFC at Thirty-second and Lexington.

She walked across the street and into the KFC. As she entered she noticed Colonel Sanders had no eyes, just black slashes behind his black glasses. She stood and stared at those black slashes until she noticed a Latina girl with braces and yellow sparkle eye makeup watching her from behind the counter. Melanie flipped her hair with the back of her hand and then ran the hand across the front of her dress, reassured by the ridges down her stomach. She used to work out on the Stairmaster in the corporate gym until she was dizzy.

She slipped into a red plastic corner booth. Melanie found herself staring at a JOIN TEAM KFC! sign above the KFC employee of the month, and she imagined herself in the back with the manager, in a room half the size of the White/Weld elevator, filling out an application for employment. She saw herself looking down at her consulting career autopsied beneath the big red "KFC" across the top of the job application. Melanie left the booth and walked to the counter. The Latina girl watched her. Melanie stared at the deep fryer in the back. She saw herself, Melanie Applebee, standing at the fryer with her hair bunched under a KFC cap, plunging chicken into sizzling oil. The girl at the counter asked her if she was OK, and Melanie spun away from the counter and walked out the glass door and into the parking lot.

She stood for a moment hyperventilating in the KFC parking lot, and then ran up and over a grass partition into the floodlit parking lots of a True Value hardware store and a Hart drugstore. Melanie Applebee had been in charge of the Hart account at White/Weld. She had been praised by Hart's management for her plan for a restructuring. The plan closed down marginal stores, bought a chain of cut-rate drugstores, slashed the pension program, reduced employee stock options, severely limited the health plan, and cut wages. A Dillon Reed associate she went on a blind date with at the time told her everything she and he were doing was probably pure evil. He said he had just figured it out at that moment, watching her gleefully describe her work on the Hart project, and he excused himself and left the restaurant.

She stood fingering her pearls and looking into the empty aisles of the Hart drugstore. A truck full of cowboys howling like dogs careened past her, and again she ran until the strip mall gave way and she was gasping beneath a reflecting glass office tower. Gold letters carved into the stone facing over the four glass revolving doors said EL PASO NATIONAL BANK. A young Latino man inside wearing a Walkman was polishing the brass around the elevators. He turned and motioned for her to go away.

Melanie started to walk away, but she walked back until she was pressed flat against the stone walls of the bank. She ran her hands over the surface of the marble facing as if over the skin of a lover, tried to melt through the warm stone, pounded her fist over and over on the office tower.

Melanie Applebee spent the night curled around the shrubbery in the center of the plaza at the base of El Paso National Bank. She awoke crying out from a nightmare, her hands clenching her pearls. She stood up and two secretaries stopped short in their path to stare. She bent down and brushed herself off. Two executives glanced over and hiccuped in their strides. Out of the corner of her eye Melanie saw a security guard swinging out through the revolving door at the front of the bank tower. Melanie ran forward through the bushes and stumbled across the red stone plaza as the security guard called out.

Melanie looked out at the honking bumper-to-bumper traffic alongside the road. She turned down an alley and quickened her steps. There was a Dumpster, and Latino men tossing rotten vegetables into it. They turned to look at her. One pointed and laughed. She had to pull herself away from the food.

Melanie asked three men directions to the library before one stopped. She followed the street signs diligently from Texas to Stanton to Franklin to Oregon. At Oregon she bent over, her hands on her knees. Her pearls banged against her chin. She fell to her knees. A line from a paper she'd written at Stanford drifted through her head: "The genius of the free market is the accuracy with which it assigns a market value to all things."

She stood and found the El Paso library in front of her. She entered, found the periodicals room, took the *El Paso–Ciudad Juárez Bulletin* off the wall rack. She had to give her body explicit instructions: Pick up the paper, open your hand, close your hand on the paper, walk over there, pull back the chair, sit, open the paper, find the classifieds. She looked down at a color photo of a small Spanish mission, the centerpiece of a page of real estate ads. The ad's text said the Senecu Mission was "one of the smaller missions strung like pearls along the former banks of the Rio Grande." She read the sentence over a dozen times until she understood they were selling a mission church. Her father had been an elder in the Greek Orthodox church of Des Moines. She found herself unable to picture her father or mother or even her childhood home in Des Moines.

A homeless man was grinning at her from across the room. She remembered she was looking for a job, decided she needed a pencil and paper, stood, and asked for them from the librarian. Words bounced around her mouth as if made of rubber. After being handed the pencil she wondered how to explain her six months out of work to a future employer. She had always grimaced at the idea of *Melanie Applebee* having an unexplained gap on her résumé. She never hired anyone who couldn't account in verifiable detail, utilizing a series of action verbs, for every corporate month of their life. She returned to her chair with the pencil gripped tightly in her hand. She looked down at the newspaper, remembered again she was looking for a job, and her blond head slipped to the table.

She awoke and wandered out of the library. She sat down on the stone front steps, saw the El Paso–Juárez Border Jumper trolley roll by, put her face in her hands, and fell asleep. When she awoke she looked up at the sun and guessed it was early afternoon. When she awoke again, she looked aimlessly at the pedestrian traffic on the street. After a couple of minutes, she thought she recognized someone. She yelled out a name, and the boy turned and came up the steps.

"Kyle," she said, too tired to care.

"Señora MBA," he said.

He bought her pearls for seventy-five dollars cash. She held them out to him with a strange relief. Kyle got her a cab, told the driver to take her to the airport La Quinta Inn, where he told her she'd get a room for free if she asked for Manuela and used his Juárez name, Carlos.

She stretched out in the back of the cab and fell asleep dreaming of eating from a smorgasbord of iced Maine, Alaskan, and Martha's Vineyard bluepoint oysters in the White/Weld executive dining hall.

Melanie Applebee slept for thirty hours at the El Paso Airport La Quinta Inn. When she awoke she reached for the clicker and found CNN's business news. The market was up another 49 points. It was about to break 6,000. She threw back the covers, jumped out of the bed. She stripped off her clothes. She lay down in the shower and let the water beat on her until her skin hurt with the pounding. She called Henry Smyth's name under her breath like a mantra. She turned the water hotter until she had to bite into the back of her forearm to keep from screaming. When Melanie came out of the bathroom it was dark.

Melanie saw the inside of the Stock Exchange on the TV, the ticker tape running like hieroglyphics across the bottom of the screen. She slapped her hands together and fell to her knees before Wall Street and bowed her head and, praying out loud, begged to be allowed to return. She walked on her knees to the TV and ran her fingers over the live shot of the Exchange, touched the tiny heads of the traders reverently with the tips of her fingers.

She washed her face, put on a new black dress and shoes from Talbot's someone had left in the room, and took the elevator downstairs. A young executive with a blond cowlick stood at the front desk in a Brooks Brothers suit. She looked straight at him, but he looked through her, as if she were a ghost. She moved sideways into his line of sight and smiled; now he looked at her, frowned, and looked away. She stood in the lobby and glared at him He glanced at her again and turned away.

Melanie was staring vacantly in the lobby with her hand on her bare neck when she saw Kyle walking through the lobby with an empty animal cage in his hand. She felt suddenly proud of him, as if he were her entrepreneurial younger brother. He spotted her and walked over.

"What was in the cage?" said Melanie.

"Selling an ocelot to some French guy," said Kyle. "Endangered species."

"An ocelot?"

"You'd not believe what the guy paid for a fucking ocelot. I nailed him for an extra five hundred in the end," Kyle said, and pointing out the door of the La Quinta, added, "Your cab, Señora." She looked at the cab, watched it pull away. He reached out and touched the bite marks on her arm with two fingers. He looked at her and said under his breath, "You'd make fuckloads in a few weeks."

"How much?"

"Fuckloads."

He looked at her blankly and then nodded and repeated, "Fuckloads." He said, reaching out to touch her arm again, "Maybe you too stupid, Señora. Go. Get in a cab and go back to New York." He walked toward the glass doors of the hotel. She remembered banging on the outside of the El Paso National Bank tower, banging as if it were an enormous stone drum, as if summoning the gods, and the idea of summoning the gods struck her as so odd she laughed out loud. People turned to look as she ran laughing across the lobby and grabbed Kyle by the shoulder. He turned as if he expected to feel her hand on his shoulder, smiled as Smyth used to smile when they took out-of-town clients to dinner and he ran his fat thumb up to her panties under the table.

"Ought to be easy for someone with an MBA," said Kyle. "All you have to do is drive a car and look like a pretty Anglo."

Melanie smiled at the mention of her MBA and he walked her by the elbow to the bar. Kyle told her he could set up the first run in a day, maybe two; rhapsodized over the easy money she'd make with each crossing of the border. The bartender, Milo, seemed to know Kyle, kept winking at him as he refilled her glass. She drank steadily, found it easy to forget what Kyle was proposing, and tried to focus on how she would use the money to return to New York on her own terms.

Kyle finally left, and she looked drunkenly at the Guatemalan boy emptying the ashtray in front of her and was filled with a delightful pity, the kind she always felt at the close of her yearly vacation on St. Lucia, when looking at the shacks of the natives on the way to the airport.

Melanie Applebee left the El Paso Airport La Quinta Inn in a limousine the next evening. She had spent the afternoon drinking Absolut in her room, sketching a business plan for her future consulting firm on hotel stationery, until she was too buzzed to do anything but doodle insects among her elaborate calculations. She suddenly checked the clock, strode fiercely if unevenly around the bed, opened the door with executive confidence, and took the elevator downstairs to wait in the lobby for the limousine.

Kyle was in a rivet-studded jean jacket in the back of the limousine with a boom box in his lap, and he poured her a glass of Veuve Clicquot champagne as they shot onto I-10 toward downtown El Paso. She laughed; it was all like a movie. She decided that someday, when her new consulting firm was a complete success, she would retire and write the screenplay of these cinematic days.

Out the tinted window of the limousine, El Paso looked like a lunar colony, and Melanie suddenly remembered spending the night in the bushes at the foot of El Paso National Bank. The limousine crossed the dark green Rio Grande on the Stanton Street bridge and stopped in the traffic for Mexican customs.

Melanie looked ahead and saw Mexican soldiers staring into windows. A carload of white men were making faces like devils into the dark windows of her limousine. She tried to twist around to see the corporate towers of El Paso, but they were behind her now. She turned to Kyle and said, "I'm in this just until I make enough to go back to Manhattan and open my own small consulting firm."

Kyle nodded and murmured, "You'll make a fuckload every run."

The Mexican customs agent looked at the limousine's plate and waved the car through without the driver even lowering the tinted window.

"They know you," said Melanie Applebee.

"Heading south," said Kyle, "they all know us."

A filthy little girl of no more than five stepped in front of the car on the Mexican side. She was selling little birds made from pipe cleaners and brilliantly colored fluff. Melanie remembered playing dress-up when she was the girl's age, wearing her mother's wedding dress and her pearls. She sat straight up at the memory, spilling her drink, and reached for the pearls missing from her neck.

The limousine driver honked, and the Mexican girl stepped slowly aside. As the limousine passed, the Mexican girl stared blankly through the dark windows into Melanie's eyes and waved the pipe-cleaner-and-fluff bird back and forth mechanically.

The limousine sped up onto the Avenida 16 de Septiembre. Kyle pointed to a huge saguaro cactus strapped to the back of a flatbed, whistled in appreciation, said it was worth thousands smuggled into the States. Coming toward them, heading to the States, an endless stream of tractor trailers, chemical trucks, gas trucks, trucks loaded with new cars: Fords, Saturns, Geos. Melanie turned all the way around in her seat to look back at the sulfurous lights of Mexican customs. She was going to be driving back through customs in twenty-four hours, in a car with a gas tank full of bagged heroin. Kyle told her she would never be stopped; her innocent Anglo face was her free pass.

The limousine took a right and she saw signs for the Rio Grande Mall, the Pueblito Mexicano Mall, and a lit billboard for the Pan American Highway. Kyle pointed out a stadium glowing in the distance and said it was used for bullfights. Melanie stared out, as if at the set for a movie, at the endless tar-paper and pallet shacks of the new *colonias*, where the tens of thousands of *maquiladoras* lived who worked for border-hopping blue-chip American companies. She had never actually seen the *colonias*. Melanie had headed a project that sent one of Save-Rite's clothing manufacturers south, where the *maquiladoras* were paid seven to twenty cents an hour. At the closing of the Save-Rite project, Melanie had made a fervent speech at the Waldorf-Astoria praising the self-regulating wisdom of the invisible hand of the international marketplace, and the logic of NAFTA in particular.

As the limousine bounced over potholes, to her surprise Melanie found tears slipping down her cheeks, and wiped them with the back of her hand. She raised her hand to look at the moisture on the back of her thumb. She couldn't remember the last time she had cried; she did remember once saying tears were an inefficient mechanism of change, and although she couldn't remember to whom this was said, or in what context, she remembered it was funny at the time.

She could feel Kyle watching her as she looked out at the *colonias*. He pushed his hips up as he dug in the pocket of his jeans. He pulled out her pearls, draped them over the back of her hand. Melanie looked down at the pearls and said, "I thought you said nothing was free." She picked up the pearls, looked at them dangling from her hand for a moment, tossed them back into Kyle's lap. He picked up the pearls, leaned over, and quickly secured them around Melanie's neck. Her skin burned where his fingers brushed her neck.

The limousine suddenly pulled to the side of the highway, near a black Ford Explorer with tinted windows, and a Mexican army officer stepped out. He climbed in next to Melanie, introduced himself as Colonel "Gary" Gonzales, poured a whiskey from the bar, and said, pointing to the roof of the limousine, "Soon you will be back up there with the angels . . . *anglos,* yes?" Melanie laughed and poured herself a glass of whiskey, and her hand shook so hard as she gulped it down that half the drink ended up between her breasts.

The desert sky flashed turquoise in the west. Yucca stood in the dusk like ghostly sentinels. The limousine rumbled into the macadam breakdown lane and turned onto the desert. Behind the limousine rose a plume of dust red from the taillights. The limousine slid to a stop next to a plane. Melanie recognized it as an old twin-prop XB3 Piper, camouflaged with the hues of the desert. She had studied the Piper Corporation at Stanford.

"Someone would like to meet you," said Colonel Gonzales. He had slid out of the limousine and spoke as he opened her door. The sky was covered with clouds like the bellies of fish. She walked stiffly as her heels sank into the desert. The warm night air clung urgently to her exposed skin. There was a small stool into the dark plane. A bat flitted by her head. She tried to step into the plane, stumbled; when Kyle grabbed her arm she slapped him, and slurred, "I can do it myself, thank you." As Melanie entered the dark cavern of the Piper she took a deep breath and imagined herself soon looking down from the floor-to-ceiling tinted windows of the new Manhattan office of Applebee Consultants.

Melanie Applebee was grabbed by her arms as she stepped into the plane's dark cabin. Someone yelled, *"No se muevan."* She was shoved down until she was sitting on the warm metal floor of the plane. A needle was drilled into her arm. An immobilizing intoxication burned through her. She was picked up and propped up against the wall. The light came on in the cabin, the door was pulled shut, and the plane rocked along the dirt runway. There was a white man with his back to her sitting in one of the few seats in the plane. She saw Colonel Gonzales sit next to him. A man moving toward her was dressed in robes, some sort of sheik. Melanie Applebee had assisted in the purchase of 262 Park Avenue by the Kuwaitis in 1989; the idea drifted in her drug-burned brain to mention this fact. Perhaps she could work as a consultant for the Kuwaitis—they would make the perfect first client.

The sheik put the back of his hand on her cheek, pushed her face from side to side. She was given another injection. It pulled the bones from her body.

"Where?" was all she could push through her numb lips.

The sheik waved his hand in dismissal, said without looking down at her, "To Mexico City, then to Oman. Or Dubai. Where the market wills." He laughed at this and pointed a silver-ringed finger at her. There was a white man sitting with his back to her in one of the few seats in the plane, reading the *Wall Street Journal*. Before she lost consciousness, she saw a graph of the stock market on the newspaper in his hands rising like a black lightning bolt.

The Battle of Khafji

I WAS A CLEAN-CUT Burlington boy who joined the marines to get money for college. I could run faster with a pack on my back than anyone else at boot camp that month, so they sent me off for recon training to be the best of the best and all I could be as the son of a tax-killed dairy farmer whose land is now suburban homes you could park a B-52 in, and for which he got shit. Recon is an elite group of soldiers. We are the guys who get sent behind enemy lines to take a look-see around before the real action starts up. We have a 90 percent casualty rate during wartime, of which we are supposed to be proud.

My Third Force recon platoon was sent to Saudi soon after Saddam entered Kuwait. We were flown over on a C-130 transport with other assorted personnel from San Francisco and didn't even know where the fuck we were heading until we were in the air. This one old gunnery sergeant was throwing ammunition around the plane like it was candy at fucking Mardi Gras. Marines normally treat ammunition like the gold in Fort Knox—you don't just throw the shit around—but it was like a party: *We were finally going to get some trigger time.* No one in my recon platoon—including Captain Beck—had ever seen any action.

A lot of us were wearing face paint as if we were going into a hot LZ. Maybe that and the general confusion accounts for this weird shit. You need to know this about Sergeant Packer right off: *The man wasn't one of us.* No one noticed when he answered during roll call to the name of Sergeant Packer. We figured it out midflight, and he told Captain Beck he *was* in fact Sergeant Packer, and then showed this stamped official TAD order. That's Temporary Additional Duty order. So there was some kind of computer screwup, and we got this Sergeant Packer, and our own, *real* Sergeant Packer, a 6'6" guy from Macon, Georgia, with a 42" vertical leap, was who the fuck knows where.

You would think Captain Beck would set it right when we landed in the Saudi, but when he found out he just wouldn't believe it. It was like it wouldn't get in his skull that the computers had fucked up big-time. He wasn't angry yet, just laughed like *there is no fucking way this shit is really happening.* The thing you have to know about Captain Laurence Beck: the man was seriously hung up on the high tech. He had been a brain on the fast track, serving as the special liaison with the Department of Defense or some such shit, when his uncle—a congressman—got the idea he needed a few combat stars for his chest before he moved up to flag rank. So they sent him to us. He was one seriously squared-away marine—I mean, he looked like a recruiting poster with the square jaw and ice blue eyes—but he was a real prick who hated to spend time with his men and read weapon manuals like some of the men read *Playboy*.

We landed in the Saudi on this two-lane road up near Ras-al-Mishab, about twenty klicks south of Khafji. People figured Captain Beck would report the screwup ASAP to Marine Expeditionary Force Headquarters, and soon we would have our old Sergeant Packer with us. But Captain Beck, he didn't report the screwup to MEF-HQ, he couldn't deal at all. It was like at first he couldn't *see* this Sergeant Packer—who was so ugly, people right away started calling something ugly *packer*. Yeah, he was that ugly. Only thing we got out of this Sergeant Packer at first was that he was in transportation—a rear job filled with dumb shits driving buses. That went over big with the platoon—he was so totally unprepared for our line of work it was comical.

In our first days in the Saudi, this Packer was in and out of the mess in two minutes. He was like a ghost—you never saw him except for those two minutes. I left my tray and followed him out one day and asked him if he had notified MEF-HQ about the situation. His little eyes went out of focus, and he looked at his feet and mumbled some shit about not interrupting the chain of command. I told him not to give me that shit and we stood there and then he reached in the pocket of his cammies and takes out this photo that is all crumpled up. It's this not-bad-looking babe with two blond kids. One is maybe two years old and the other is maybe twelve. He tells me he was an asshole and walked out on them a few months earlier and the little kid grabbed some wires in their unfinished apartment and electrocuted himself, and then his wife hooked up with this fucked-up marine who stole a humvee and drove them into a head-on. His wife and the twelve-year-old died in the humvee crash. What do you say to that? He took the photo back and he's looking around at the desert and I'm understanding: this Packer doesn't give a fuck anymore.

That night at chow I told the platoon what I knew about how this Sergeant Packer walked out on his family and how they all got killed. People nodded at this, but shit like that happened all the time. People were more interested in Corporal Maclean and how he and some of the others had noticed this Sergeant Packer had a weird effect on mechanicals. Corporal Maclean said that morning he was cleaning his M-16 and Packer walked by and the thing jammed with sand. He said he cleaned out the sand and saw Packer go into the shitter. When Packer came out of the shitter, Corporal Maclean said Sergeant Packer looked at the M-16 and the thing jammed again, jammed so bad it took him hours to get it working cleanly.

Sergeant Vito turned from the end of the table. Vito is this bear of a guy, drinks only milk, never says shit to anyone. I figured he'd tell Maclean he was fucked, but instead he said he was lying on his rack listening to his Walkman that afternoon, and Sergeant Packer went by the window, and bang, the batteries died. I asked him, when's the last time you changed the batteries, fucking Stateside? Sergeant Vito told me they were fucking Duracells and he put them in just that morning.

This sort of shit spreads like wildfire, and by the next evening at mess everyone had a report about some mechanical breaking down in the vicinity of Sergeant Packer. Corporal Maclean was keeping tabs on the rumors, jumping from table to table. And right then Sergeant Packer walked into the mess. I had the feeling he had been outside the door for a while, listening to this shit. He came in and he looked around the room, he looked at us, and it was like he was seeing us for the first time. He just stood in the door blinking like he was waking up from a dream, and then he ate with his back to us. But after he ate he didn't bolt from the mess. He sat there and one by one we all left until the fat little fuck was left in there all alone. I was the second to last to leave the mess. Corporal Maclean was the last, and asshole that he was, he turned off the lights on Sergeant Packer.

The platoon kept talking about this weird effect of Sergeant Packer on mechanicals for the next few weeks. It was just starting to die out when this shit happened with Captain Beck. I figured Beck had to have heard the rumors about Sergeant Packer, but an officer who can't accept that computers fuck up is not an officer who can accept a sergeant can affect mechanicals. Anyway, I stepped out of the mess after lunch, and right across the street is this concrete barracks where Captain Beck bunked. Down the street I noticed Sergeant Packer coming toward the mess. Captain Beck comes out of his barracks with Corporal Acheson and the two jump into a humvee, but the fucking humvee won't start. Corporal Acheson gets out, looks under the hood. At first Captain Beck is giving Corporal Acheson some shit and then he turns and sees Sergeant Packer giving the humvee this killer stare. Captain Beck gets out and looks from Packer at the humvee and back again and then turns and goes back into his hootch. There is this silence in the street, and Corporal Acheson sits in the humvee and shakes his head at me.

That night I moved over in the mess and asked Sergeant Packer if he knew about the rumors about him and mechanicals breaking down. He shrugs his shoulders like *who gives a fuck* and keeps shoveling potatoes into his face. He stopped once with the potatoes in midair to remind me his wife and kid were killed in a stolen humvee. It looks like he's put ten more pounds on his fat little body in the Saudi. Right then a siren goes off and it was our first biological alert and we all grabbed the rubber masks off our thighs and pulled them over our crew-cut heads and some of us—including me—freaked and plunged the atropine syringes into our thighs. We all sat there looking at each other like a bunch of insects. Except for Sergeant Packer. He didn't put on his mask, just kept shoveling potatoes into his fat face.

We spent at least a couple of hours late each afternoon sitting by the side of the road behind the cinder-block barracks on boxes of M-60 ammo, watching for the rare vehicle, reading the *Arabic News,* counting the incoming helo-53 transports, and sipping shoe polish filtered through four slices of bread for the alcohol. We were sitting there pretty rocked one day when we see this Saudi bus barreling up the hardball. It was a company of Saudi marines, they got out and stood around blinking suspiciously. HQ thought our platoon wasn't doing much at Ras-al-Mishab except waiting to be sent up to Khafji and begin our infiltrations of Kuwait, so someone at HQ got the bright idea we should train these Saudi marines. And not just train them, but train them for the cameras from the Marine Historical Division, so there would be an official record of how Saudis and Americans all worked together during Desert Shield.

First thing Captain Beck orders is a simple helo snatch for the Historical Division movie cameras. We radio south to Saphiniya for a helo and take one of the Achmeds—we called all the Saudis Achmed or Al Wadi—out in the desert a ways. Ten minutes later the helo rotors overhead and drops a line and we hook on the Saudi soldier and up he goes dangling into the sky. The cameras are rolling, and all our necks are bent back as we watch the Saudi flailing around up there screaming like a lamb to the fucking slaughter. The helicopter took him in a circle, and then went behind the barracks, and when it zoomed overhead again the Saudi was dangling a couple of dozen feet overhead and still screaming like a motherfucker.

The platoon looked up at the Screaming Saudi in the Sky, and one by one we started to crack up. Captain Beck wasn't laughing, and you could see on his face the Saudi soldier disgusted him. Just before the helo set down the Saudi and he started kissing the sand, I saw Captain Beck eyeballing Sergeant Packer, and that was when I noticed Sergeant Packer wasn't laughing either. I went over and stood next to Sergeant Packer and he said to me that for the last couple of months he had dreamed about dangling just like that from a helicopter. I didn't ask him, he just told me, and then he turned like he was heading back to the barracks, and that was when Captain Beck yelled out for Sergeant Packer to lead the Saudis in a rifle drill.

Everyone in the platoon turned to look at Captain Beck. First of all, we all had the idea Captain Beck didn't even know Sergeant Packer was on the face of the planet. Second, here he was asking the fat little bus driver to lead a rifle drill for the Marine Historical Division cameras when our own Corporal Zellman was once on the Presidential Honor Guard. Then the rest of the platoon started to snicker, figuring Captain Beck wanted to make Sergeant Packer look like an asshole. I wasn't laughing, because I had the idea Captain Beck didn't think just Packer was an asshole, but all of us.

Sergeant Packer ran out there in front of the cameras. It was the first time I had seen Packer move faster than a dead man's walk, and you could see the rolls of fat under his uniform. Sergeant Packer took a long time organizing the Saudis into three rows and then all of a sudden some Saudi soldier started to yodel off on a dune and the Saudis had to take a break to get down on the sand on their knees and pray toward

Mecca. The way he was looking at the Saudis, I had the idea for a split second Packer was going to get down on the ground and pray right along with them.

Finally the prayers were over and Packer got the Saudis in line and stood in front of them, looking kind of confused, and had them affix bayonets. He slowly thrust his bayonet toward us as the cameras from the Marine Historical Division rolled. The thrust was kind of weak, and the Saudis behind him were waving their bayonets all over the fucking place. Someone started to laugh, and then Sergeant Packer took another step toward us, and from then on his routine started to get crisp. His eyes opened wide, and he almost looked afraid, as if he didn't know what was coming over him. Behind him the three rows of Saudi marines were like Abbot and Costello in their attempts to mirror him. The Saudis tried to scalp each other, but Sergeant Packer was suddenly making these razor cuts with his bayonet, like he was cutting through the skin of time. It wasn't just me, I heard Corporal Zellman, who as I said was on the Presidential Honor Guard, whisper, "He's fucking beautiful, man. Packer's speaking the language, man, loud and clear. Nobody speaks that language anymore."

One who didn't like the language Packer was speaking was Captain Beck. I looked over at him and he was looking at Packer like he wanted to rip his head off. He saw me looking and he turned around and headed back to the barracks. The rest of the platoon stood looking at Sergeant Packer, knowing for a fact we had just seen someone do something far better than should have been possible, and then Corporal Zellman tried to high-five Sergeant Packer, but the little man just looked at him with a look like *get fucked* and walked out into the desert.

The next day the call came from Marine Expeditionary Force HQ that we were to proceed up the coast to the Persian Gulf beach resort town of Khafji. We dropped off some of our extra gear in a condo in Khafji after Corporal Zellman shot off the lock like in the movies, and then we moved right up to the goddamn Kuwaiti border. Saudis had a big sand berm twenty feet high that ran the whole border with Kuwait, with big concrete fortresses every thousand yards or so that we called the Alamos. Saudi border guards called the *salaladud* were in the Alamos in normal times to keep out the infidels. No sign of those Saudi fuckers now. We sat around that first night spitting chew on the sand rats' oriental rugs in the downstairs tearoom of one of the Alamos, thinking about you all back home trimming your Christmas trees and singing hallelujah. We were at the head of the spear now, as nobody else was this close to the Iraqis in the whole Desert Storm operation.

It was out of the Alamos that we would run our recon patrols into Iraqi-occupied Kuwait, but first we just ran a couple of warm-up missions along the Saudi–Kuwait border. We were on our way back to the Alamo after one of these missions when a black cloud rolled across the barrier plain between us and Kuwait. You could see it coming, this thick black fog. In the distance you could hear some serious explosions. We walked on, but in a couple of minutes it was lights out, total darkness in the middle of the fucking day. You couldn't see your hand in front of your face. There were six of us in the patrol, including Sergeant Packer, who Captain Beck insisted come along with us.

Sergeant Zabrinski started going on about how the oil fields had been hit big time, and Sergeant Vergil Anderson, who was some sort of born-again freak, started in about how this was the end of the world and how the Lord was coming to judge us. Nobody said anything to that, because it *was* like the end of the world. Zabrinski broke the silence and gave Vergil Anderson some shit like, *What if your man already came, realized he couldn't do shit, and got the fuck out of here?* Vergil Anderson started to freak out, and that's when Sergeant Packer said sort of out of nowhere, *"Nobody's coming."* It was weird to hear Sergeant Packer speak, weirder still in the fucking darkness, and everyone shut up and thought their own thoughts and listened to our bombs raining down over there in Kuwait like it was the Fourth of July.

The desert was shaking under our feet. I don't know how much time passed, but the acrid smoke started to lift, and then we saw lights moving toward us from the direction of Kuwait. Sergeant Zabrinski hissed, and we slipped to the sand. There were voices speaking in Arabic, they were walking right toward us.

The Iraqis fell to their knees and threw up their hands crying, "Inshallah!" when we moved on them. We pushed them to the deck and tied their hands behind their heads with 5-50 parachute cord. Some were shaved bald and others had freaky-kinky hair.

We marched the Iraqis back to the Alamo. These were only the first of the Iraqi deserters, as time went by they'd be coming across the barrier plain by the hundreds. When we got back to the Alamo, Captain Beck told us to take their boots for our infiltrations. We took the Iraqis' boots so we would leave their treads in the sand when we slipped over the border and walked around Kuwait. When we took off their boots, we saw their feet, which were all seriously messed up with sores and blisters, in part because only one of them had any socks. There was a lot of oozing yellow pus, and their feet stank up the Alamo. Later that night the Marine POW translators showed up along with an intelligence officer, and the Iraqis were brought into a back room of the Alamo and questioned one by one. I was in there, and the Iraqis told a consistent story of an army without food, supplies, means of communication, or the desire to fight. They told how they saw whole platoons of Iraqi soldiers buried alive under the sand by our bombs.

One of the Iraqi prisoners looked about twelve and was too scared to speak. When I came out with the last prisoner, there was Sergeant Packer sitting in the center of the floor of the Alamo, cleaning the feet of the twelve-year-old. He had a bucket of water, and by his knee was a bottle of peroxide, and in his hand a gauze pad. The kid's feet were seriously fucked up, and strewn around were crumpled gauze pads with yellow secretions and bloodstains.

Captain Beck came out of the rear room with the translators and stopped in his tracks and stared at Sergeant Packer's back. He told Packer to ready the prisoners for transport, but Packer went on wiping the Iraqi kid's feet. Captain Beck went over and kicked over the bucket of water. It spread out under the asses of the Iraqi prisoners, but they were looking at Captain Beck's pissed-off face and didn't move a muscle. Sergeant Packer went on cleaning the kid's feet, but now the kid was scared and pulled his feet out of Packer's hands and scuttled backward across the floor, yammering in Arabic. Then all the Iraqis started yelling at Sergeant Packer, waving him off. The Iraqis settled down finally, the translators went outside, but Captain Beck kept staring at Sergeant Packer's back like he wanted to take out his sidearm and pop a round into the back of his head. Captain Beck finally went outside, and the prisoners just stared at Sergeant Packer, who took out a candy bar and opened it up and offered it to the twelve-year-old Iraqi, but the kid kept shaking his head. He probably figured Sergeant Packer wanted to poison him. It was only later I remembered

Sergeant Packer's own kid was about twelve when he died in the humvee wreck.

We had a bunch of supersnooper and night-vision scopes set up all in a row on the roof of the Alamo and could look right over and see Iraqis beyond the mines and concertina wire of the barrier plain. When you looked through the scopes at the minefield, the first thing you noticed were the camel parts strewn all over. The Bedouin left them and the mines blew them up. So we were up on the roof, and Captain Beck was adjusting one of the scopes and turned to me and said, "So, who do you think we should send over there first?"

My first thought was, *You motherfucker.* I was right, he was thinking of sending Sergeant Packer. After the thing with the Iraqis' feet, Packer was on his shit list. But the whole idea was fucked. It was one thing keeping Packer around as a mascot, it was another to send him on a night infiltration of enemy-occupied territory. I pointed out Packer was from transportation and a fat fuck and that we had all had specialized training in the Mojave, but Captain Beck didn't hear a word. He went off on how *the satellites* could get *a chimpanzee* through that minefield, how *the satellites* could get a fucking *Iraqi* through the minefield, how *the satellites* could certainly get *fucking Packer* through the minefield. An F-18 flew over on the way to bomb Baghdad, and he started giving me a lecture about how *fucking beautiful* the plane was, and I pretty much left him up there talking to himself.

Six marines, including the bus driver Sergeant Packer, set off that night for a 48-hour infiltration of Kuwait. There was some talk of how fucked it was to have Packer along, but no one was ready to go over Captain Beck's head. The six marines were all wearing night-vision goggles and one-piece tan desert flight suits that Corporal Fallow had scammed from the quartermaster. Sergeant Zabrinski held the Global Positioning Satellite unit. The GPS unit would guide them through the Iraqi minefield. All they had to do was follow the directions on the glowing readout from the little box in Zabrinski's hand. They would be led by a satellite in the sky.

The six stepped out into the dark and switched on their night-vision goggles. It is like looking through the eyes of a fly. Everything is phosphorescent green, and human beings leave hazy green trails behind them as they move across your field of vision. I pulled the iron gate of the Alamo down behind them and then went up on the roof of the Alamo to watch through the Quester scope as they made their way toward the mined barrier plain. We saw Sergeant Zabrinski raise his hand as the six infiltrators closed in on the minefield. He hand-motioned for the marines to set up an initial rally point: a 360-degree circle of men facing outboard. It was a moment to sit, listen, adjust gear, orient to the sounds of the night. Sergeant Zabrinski stood up, looked at the GPS in his hand, took two steps to the left, then three steps forward. The other men followed his tracks. We all held our breath, as I don't think anyone—except Captain Beck—had total faith in the GPS. Captain Beck didn't even come up on the roof of the Alamo. I went downstairs and found him making tea. He said to me, "Packer was in need of some attitude adjustment. Kuwait will tenderize him."

I left Captain Beck stirring his tea and went back upstairs and looked through the Quester scope for the infiltrators. They were on the far side of the barrier plain. I sat down on the roof and looked up at the sky and tried to spot the satellite that was leading them through the mines. After that I stretched out on the roof of the Alamo and fell asleep. I remember I dreamed about being in college—which, as I said already, is what I joined the marines to get money for—and then I had a nightmare about Captain Beck. Some sort of commotion in front of the Alamo was what woke me up. It was Vergil Anderson. He had captured a photographer with Agence France-Presse. The photographer had broken away from a press pool that night and walked the twenty klicks from Ras-al-Mishab. He was seriously dehydrated and delusional. He wanted to walk to Kuwait and from there to Baghdad to document the effects of our bombing. Captain Beck had me and Vergil Anderson hydrate him and bind his hands with the plastic flexcuffs we reserved for Iraqi POWs and deliver him to MEF-HQ in the rear. He pissed on us all the way to MEF-HQ about our bombing and told us how our hands were permanently bloodied and how it was just high-tech slaughter and all that sort of bullshit.

We did some other details at MEF-HQ, came back the next evening. When we came in the Alamo, we found Captain Beck watching the RPV monitor in the tearoom. The RPV is this Remotely Piloted Vehicle—a mechanical bird with a camera in its guts. Captain Beck was looking through the bird's eye at the Iraqi positions just over the mined barrier plain. As I looked at the monitor I saw the mechanical bird was flying low over an Iraqi digging frantically into a sand dune, his tail up in the air. Captain Beck mimed the Iraqi's frantic burrowing, and laughed like he owned the fucking world until he saw me and Vergil Anderson looking at him. I nudged Vergil Anderson and we went up on the roof and looked through the Quester at the barrier plain. It was still daytime, so the infiltration team was still hiding over there in their wormholes in the sand, and there wasn't much to see of interest.

That night the infiltration team was three hours late. In general, they were not allowed outbound communications while in-country, as that would put them at risk of detection.

We tried to raise them with burst pulse, a relatively safe form of high-frequency communication we reserved for emergencies, but there was no response. We sat around the Alamo, waiting for Captain Beck to alert MEF-HQ so they would send in an emergency extraction team, but he just sat there drinking the Saudis' tea. Corporal Anderson finally spotted the infiltration team with the Quester scope making their way very slowly back through the mines.

Captain Beck came up on the roof, and then Corporal Maclean, looking through a TOW sight, started to freak. He said over and over, "Shit, Sergeant Packer's walking point." Everyone ran to one of the scopes to take a look at this, and when I got my eye on a scope, sure enough there was fat little Sergeant Packer, about three meters ahead of the rest of the men. When the infiltration team came closer I noticed this: Sergeant Packer didn't have the GPS in his hand. The bus driver was leading them freestyle. When I turned from the TOW sight to point this out, Captain Beck was gone from the roof of the Alamo. The rest of us stood up there watching, expecting at any second to see the infiltration team blown to Kingdom Come.

The team made it back to the Alamo. It turned out the GPS and the other electronics had gone down over there, and Sergeant Packer had volunteered to lead them back. He had followed old camel tracks through the mines. You could see the other five men who went on the infiltration had no more doubts about Sergeant Packer. You put your dick on the line like that, you're one of us. Sure, the men were spooked by Sergeant Packer, about how maybe his weird effect on mechanicals had caused the GPS to go down. But no one was talking much about that right then.

Captain Beck was only interested in the coordinates for the Iraqi bunkers and installations brought back by the infiltration team. We all went in and sat around the tearoom and listened to their report. Sergeant Packer turned to me and gave me a bite of chocolate bar, and then out of the fucking blue he started to sing "Silent Night." Sergeant Packer had a beautiful voice. His regular voice—although I had heard maybe two complete sentences—was like he got a tonsillectomy with a buzz saw, but when he sang it was this almost female thing, all high and sweet.

Captain Beck had his head down over his notes, and it looked like he was going to let Sergeant Packer sing. Christmas had passed us by about three weeks earlier without anyone feeling the urge to break into "Deck the Halls." When a couple of the other men suddenly started to join in, Captain Beck raised his head and said, "Shut the fuck up, Packer." But Packer didn't shut up. He just sang on and on, although he sang alone. Captain Beck looked right at him the whole time, and then when he was done Beck put on this sort of sick smile and said we'd meet back here at 0500 to complete the report.

So it was six hours later, and we were all back in the tearoom. The report was over in an hour, and then Captain Beck had Corporal Fitch get on the communicator and order up an A-10 jet. Captain Beck was the only one of us who seemed pumped up. He went chuckling over to the fun little Christmas toy known as the MULE. It stands for Multi-Utility Laser Engager. It's a plastic box with a laser beam inside. Captain Beck took the PRC-77 communicator handset and read in the coordinates for the Iraqi bunker.

While we waited for the jet, Captain Beck looked like he was about to get a blow job from Miss America. Six minutes later we saw the A-10 jet inbound from the Persian Gulf. The pilot called in for the *sparkle*, and Captain Beck turned on the laser from the MULE. The laser beam would guide the bombs from the jet to the Iraqi bunker. The A-10 popped upward and then rolled over and dove toward the target. There was a puff of smoke in the desert, and the echo of the explosion in our ribcages. Captain Beck pumped his fist and yelled, "Bingo." The bombs were Mark-84s, two thousand pounds of explosive each.

Four more two-thousand-pound bombs were dropped on Iraqi positions that morning, based on the recommendations of the returning infiltration team. I thought it was all over, and then Captain Beck said he wanted one more and called in the coordinates. After setting up the MULE he turned to Sergeant Packer with this big smile and asked him to do the honors and turn on the laser as soon as the A-10 was inbound. He told Sergeant Packer it was like a video game. Sergeant Packer just shook his head. He then refused Captain Beck's *direct order* to push the red button on the MULE. The A-10 went around a second time and Sergeant Zabrinski turned on the laser.

I expected Captain Beck would send Sergeant Packer south for a court martial for refusing a direct order, but instead Beck just left the roof of the Alamo without another word. The smile was long gone from his face, and—this is fucked—for the first time he even looked kind of worried. The other members of the platoon milled around confused, expecting something more, but when nothing happened they drifted downstairs. Sergeant Packer stood at the edge of the Alamo for a long time scanning the desert with the Quester sight. He looked out at that desert for a couple of hours, and then he lay down on the roof and fell asleep. He probably hadn't slept at all while he was on the infiltration. I sat up there with him with my back against the edge of the Alamo for the rest of the day. As the sun set, I thought how hard it was to believe a bunch of Achmeds were dead or dying over there in the sand because of us, and I decided they ought to call this Operation Video Game. I thought he was still sleeping, but then Sergeant Packer sat up and said to me out of the blue, *"Is it still a war if nobody dies on one side?"*

I said, "What?" or "Huh?" as if I didn't understand, because he was getting philosophical and in those days thinking made me feel like a faggot, and he said, "I mean, if thousands die on one side, and nobody at all dies on the other, is that still a *war*? Maybe we should have a new *word* for it?"

I said as if I was pissed, "But the war hasn't happened yet." Sergeant Packer stood up and, staring at one of our Cobra helicopters rotoring through a blazing sunset, said, "The dead are as good as dead."

Sergeant Packer and I sat up there on the roof of the Alamo long after the sun set that day. Dozens of oil fires were leaping two hundred feet into the air across the distant Kuwaiti horizon. It was like hell was right over the border. Neither of us had spoken for hours and it was silent up there except for the sizzle of desert sand blowing against the side of the Alamo. I stood up at one point and with a scope spotted one of our Cobra helos sniffing around out there over the Kuwait border, as if curious about the day's Iraqi toll.

It was as if I were keeping Sergeant Packer company in the last hours before some sort of shit finally hit the fan. And then the shit finally did hit the fan. Sergeant Packer hadn't moved a muscle in hours, and then out of the blue he jumped up and started scanning the mined barrier plain through a Quester scope. I stood up and looked through another scope. It took me a long time to locate what he was seeing, but then I saw movement on the far side of the mined barrier plain.

Neither of us had spoken a word, but as if they smelled something going down, Sergeant Zabrinski came up on the roof of the Alamo, followed by Captain Beck. Sergeant Zabrinski and Captain Beck both went right to a scope. Captain Beck turned away from his scope after spotting the figure in the minefield and glanced at me, and I swear he was grinning. I put my eye to one of the TOW sights again and watched the figure making its way through the mines. When I raised my eyes from the TOW sight and turned around, Sergeant Packer was gone from the roof of the Alamo. Thirty seconds later we saw him running across the desert in front of the Alamo toward the minefield. I looked over at Captain Beck, and he shook his head at me, like he now expected nothing less than this sort of crazy shit from Sergeant Packer.

About fifteen seconds later Sergeant Zabrinski identified the figure out there in the mined barrier plain as a *female*. I looked again through the TOW scope, and it did now look like the figure coming slowly through the mines toward Sergeant Packer was covered from head to toe. Sergeant Packer was now in the minefield, making his way toward this Arab female. It was right about then that Sergeant Zabrinski picked up on his scope a Cobra helo bearing back from the Kuwaiti horizon on a definite course for this developing situation in the minefield. Captain Beck raised his hand, pointed in the direction of the oncoming helo, and said something under his breath to Sergeant Zabrinski, who started laughing.

The Cobra helo was now the only thing moving quickly out there, and soon you could see through the scope it was clearly bearing down on this Arab female. The Cobra helicopter reads human heat on its thermal sights and destroys. The only way to avoid it is to lie down on the ground and pretzel into a non-human shape, so maybe you get read as a plant or something nonhuman. So through the scopes we saw Sergeant Packer waving his arms like he was telling the Arab female to stop and lie down, but of course she was freaked by him, and just doubled her pace through the mines.

So Packer started waving his arms at the incoming Cobra helo. The helo didn't bear off the Arab female at his waving, and I expected it to open up on her with its nose gun at any second. Sergeant Packer must have thought the same thing, because he took out his .45 and started firing at the helo, and then the big whacking insect forgot the Arab female, who stopped in her tracks. The helo swung sharply around and bore down on Sergeant Packer. It bore down on him in slow motion, as Packer emptied his .45's clip. It was pretty clear he was firing for effect, and not just throwing rounds up near the helo. You could hear the little *pop, pop, pop* from Packer's .45 over the drone of the rotor blades.

Sergeant Packer popped another clip into his .45, raised his arm again, and squeezed off round after round toward the helo. The helo was about a hundred yards away when it responded with a long burst from its 20mm nose gun. There were strings of orange tracers all over the night. The desert all around Sergeant Packer was being pocked up by 28mm rounds, but he stood his ground and fired off the last of his clip toward the helo. It was right then the helo ripped off another burst from its nose gun, and I saw Sergeant Packer take a serious hit. His body shook like he was electrocuted, and he spun around and dropped to his knees, and then tumbled over face first into the desert. The helo fired again, another spray of orange tracers, and Sergeant Packer's body twisted on the desert floor as he took at least one more hit. The helo hovered in victory over his body for about ten seconds, and then banked and headed back into the dark over the Persian Gulf. With the helo gone, you could hear the desert sand blowing against the side of the Alamo.

The silence was broken by the Arab female screaming out there in the minefield. She really let loose with her Arab lungs—it was a serious death wail she was doing out there. She was wailing and picking her way through the mines toward the body of Sergeant Packer. When she first started wailing, I unglued my eye from the TOW scope and scanned the roof of the Alamo, and that was when I noticed Captain Beck. He was not looking through a scope. He looked like the cat that finally ate the motherfucking canary. He saw me looking at him, and shaking his head said, "Not a good idea to fuck with those helo jockeys."

I didn't want to look at Captain Beck's face so I put my eye back to the TOW scope. Most of the platoon was already down there running across the desert in front of the Alamo toward the minefield. The Arab female was still making her way toward Sergeant Packer's body through the mines and still wailing. She was about five meters away from his body. It was going to be tricky extracting her and Packer's body from the minefield. It was while I was thinking about that extraction—that was when I saw little fucking Sergeant Packer out there in no-man's-land move his arm. There was no motion for another ten seconds, and then Packer's arm raised up a few inches again off the desert floor. Zabrinski, looking through another scope, saw the same motion and started to yell, and I raised my head from the TOW scope and said, "Captain Beck, better take another look."

Sergeant Packer was up and stumbling through the minefield by the time I came down from the Alamo to the edge of the

barrier plain. It was pretty clear his left leg had been clipped—
he was dragging it. By hand signals he kept the Arab woman
about three yards back as he picked their way out of the minefield. I played a flashlight over Packer's face when he made it
out of the minefield. A flap of skin was hanging down over one
eyebrow, and you could see about three inches of the white of
his skull. Blood was flowing steadily from the wound over his
face, and he had to keep blinking to see us. The cammies of his
left leg were torn up and black with blood.

With a couple of the men, Sergeant Zabrinski started to
hustle the Arab woman back toward the Alamo. She was clutching a blanket to her chest with both arms and still wailing like
it was the fucking end of the world. Sergeant Packer pushed
past us when he saw Zabrinski and the others moving the Arab
woman away, and without a word stumbled after them. Half
the platoon tried to give Packer a hand on the way back to the
Alamo, but the little bus driver cursed like a motherfucker
when anyone touched him. Eventually the platoon fell back a
few yards and just trailed behind Packer as he stumbled along.
He wasn't moving too fast, and we fell way behind Zabrinski
and the others with the Arab woman.

When we finally entered the Alamo, Captain Beck and
Sergeant Zabrinski were standing with their backs to us in front
of the Arab woman in the tearoom. Captain Beck was trying to
get a baby in a blanket out of her arms, and she was giving him
an earful of high-decibel Arabic. Neither Sergeant Zabrinski nor
Captain Beck turned around as we all followed behind Sergeant
Packer. They might not have even heard us walking toward
them behind Sergeant Packer—the Arab woman was screaming that loud as Captain Beck tugged at the baby in the blanket.

Sergeant Packer fell against Captain Beck, a kind of stumbling body block from behind. Sergeant Zabrinski immediately

swung around with his K-Bar knife out, but then backed off. Sergeant Packer reached down and took the baby in the blanket out of the arms of the Arab woman. The Arab woman just let Sergeant Packer remove it from her arms, and she stopped screaming and was silent for about ten seconds, and then started in with the waterworks. The rest of the platoon kind of melted away then. But I stood there, which is why I ended up the one to handcuff Sergeant Packer. Captain Beck didn't—or couldn't—look twice at Sergeant Packer holding the Arab baby, just walked to the tearoom and came out and handed me the plastic flexcuffs, and told Zabrinski to arrange for Packer's transport to MEF-HQ for a court martial, and then disappeared up to the roof of the Alamo.

It was with my own two hands that I put the flexcuffs on Sergeant Packer's wrists. He held out his wrists while still holding the baby in his arms. The blanket fell open as he held out his hands, and I saw that there wasn't much left below the shoulders of the baby. I heard a rumor later that the Arab woman had come all the way from Baghdad to show the remains to us.

Sergeant Packer wouldn't let anyone dress his wounds. He just stood there cuffed, holding the remains of the Iraqi baby with blood dripping down his face. The Iraqi woman finally stopped her waterworks, took the pressure bandages, gauze, scissors, and tape off the table, and wrapped his head and leg. Sergeant Zabrinski then drove the Iraqi woman and Sergeant Packer and the baby's remains in a humvee down the hardball to Marine Expeditionary Force HQ. Captain Beck had wanted to send them separately, but the Iraqi woman now wouldn't leave Sergeant Packer's side.

Sergeant Zabrinski told me later it took him and three MPs to get the Iraqi baby's remains away from Sergeant Packer when they arrived at MEF-HQ. A Colonel Herman there had

Sergeant Packer put in wrist-to-ankle shackles, and had a medic inject him with a sedative that the medic said would have put down a horse. The injection didn't knock out little Sergeant Packer. He just sat there at MEF-HQ in shackles with a face covered in dried blood, giving his *who gives a fuck* look to all the brass walking by, until they finished the paperwork and took him away.

A month later we won Desert Storm by driving the twenty klicks to Kuwait. Captain Beck was awarded a bronze star for valor. I got home and watched all the ticker-tape parades and instant replays of our great victory on the tube. Over the next year, my hands curled up into claws with arthritis and they tell me it's my imagination. I had a kid with this great woman, and the kid was born with veins on the outside of his face, and they say it's unrelated to Desert Storm.

I wake up every night now with my claws over my eyes. In the dream that wakes me up we're eating MREs in the Alamo when there is a biological warning. We pull on our gas masks and look around at each other like a bunch of insects. It is then that Sergeant Zabrinski, in his gas mask, beckons us outside. Riding toward the Alamo is this soldier without a gas mask on a camel. This soldier on a camel rides right up to us like a fucking Bedouin and motions for us to take off our gas masks, but we raise our M-16s and chase the soldier off into the desert.

PS
3566
AJ42
S33
2000
―――――――――
C.2